The Christmas Star

CHRISTOPHER FAHY

The Christmas Star

CHRISTOPHER FAHY

Overlook Connection Press
— 2012 —

THE CHRISTMAS STAR

Text © 2012 by Christopher Fahy

Cover and interior art © 2012 by Cortney Skinner

This edition is Published and © 2012 by
Overlook Connection Press
PO Box 1934, Hiram, Georgia 30141
www.overlookconncction.com
overlookcn@aol.com

First Trade Paperback Edition
ISBN-13: 978-1-62330-000-5

Book Design & Typesetting:
David G. Barnett/Fat Cat Graphic Design
www.fatcatgraphicdesign.com

To the spirit of Annabel Si Wan Fahy,
September 3, 2002—March 29, 2005,
the little visitor who couldn't stay.

The Christmas Star

Chapter 1

*Pull your bow back too far
and it will break.
Hone your blade too much
and it will lose its edge.
Constantly thirst for more
and you will never have enough.*
                              —Tao Te Ching

As soon as Dodge passed the sign that said "LEAVING DARBY — COME AGAIN" the snow began to fall. For a while it looked like the early prediction he'd seen on TV at the Fireside Inn would come to pass; the storm would amount to nothing but flurries before blowing out to sea. But then to his great chagrin the flakes increased in size and volume, and now they were coming down heavy and fast, racing straight at his windshield.

Yesterday, on his way to the inn, he had taken the turnpike and Route 48, but now that the deal was done, he was driving along the winding road that skirted the base of Sheffield Peak. This morning the Peak had belonged to a dying old man, but now it belonged to *him,* and he wanted to look at it one more time before heading back to Manhattan.

The Peak was the sweetest piece of real estate that Dodge had ever come across. It had been in the same Maine family forever; its forests were practically virgin. Dodge had been after it for years, but thinking he'd never get it, he'd finally decided to pick up a shabby resort in New Hampshire and totally renovate it. He didn't really like the idea, since even after months of costly and frustrating work, the place still wouldn't be perfect—and Dodge was a perfectionist.

The Peak was ideal for his temperament. He would have a blank slate, could do things the very best way from the start, and once he was finished, he'd own the finest ski resort in Maine. He'd put Deep Valley and Shoehorn to shame. As a matter of fact, he might even put them out of business. Lighting a cigarette, he thought: *Now wouldn't that be too bad.*

Word of his project had already spread through Darby and nearby towns, and his realtor, Jessup, had told him that some of the locals were pretty upset. They claimed he would "ruin" the Peak. Ridiculous! Nothing was there, so how could you ruin nothing? His project would not just transform that nothing into a fabulous something, it would transform the whole sad local economy too, as his critics would soon find out.

The radio was playing some music he didn't like. He punched its buttons, trying to get a weather report, but had no luck.

He drove more slowly, squinting through the windshield. The crest of the mountain was lost in the falling snow, which seemed to be intensifying. He hit the radio's "seek" button; digital numbers flew by without stopping. Reception in this wilderness was practically nonexistent.

His car was the only one on the road right now, and he drove even slower, staring at the mountain's base this time. He thought he was close to the spot where the new access road would go, but wasn't sure. He'd seen the existing single lane dirt road—which he would expand into two lane asphalt—a couple of times, remembered it lay at the foot of a hill, but which hill? This road was basically nothing but ups and downs.

He glanced at the clock on the dash. Time was slipping away. If the snow kept going like this, he could miss his plane, which would mess things up for tomorrow, his meeting with Martin & Stern about the new ad campaign for Tamarack, his lakeside resort in Vermont.

The pain in his stomach began again. The pills that he took to ease it were in his black cashmere jacket, which lay on the seat behind him. Just cool it, relax, he told himself, and took another drag on his cigarette.

In Darby he'd tried to call Paula but got her machine again, so he left a message saying he'd closed the deal, he was starting out, he ought to be back in his condo by seven. He asked her to make reservations at Romulus for tomorrow night so they could celebrate his coup in style. "Call them as soon as you get this," he told her. "You know what that place is like on Christmas Eve."

He'd remembered then that he still hadn't bought her a present. They didn't make a big deal out of Christmas but always went out on Christmas Eve and gave each other a gift. He wanted to get Paula something unique, maybe something from Maine, but there wasn't enough time to do any shopping now. He'd have to look around tomorrow at home.

A sudden rush of snow hit the windshield, jolting him out of his thoughts. "Flurries," he muttered and snuffed out his cigarette in the ashtray. Better try Paula again, let her know that he might be late. Or that maybe the Bangor flights would be grounded, God forbid, and he wouldn't be back till tomorrow.

One hand on the steering wheel, he punched the cell phone's programmed button—and was greeted by nothing but static. Pathetic. He'd try again later, but might have to be content to call from the airport. The pain in his stomach slid up a notch.

Taking a long deep breath and letting it out—*relax, relax*—he looked back at the mountain, now black in the snow and the rapidly failing light. Magnificent, really *prime!*

The guy who had owned it till just a few hours ago, an old dude named Somerset Fletcher, was gravely ill and lived in a nursing home. Joe Jessup, the local realtor Dodge had been working with these past few years, a transplant from Manhattan, had said the old codger would never sell. But then, the day before Thanksgiving, Dodge got a call in his midtown office:

"Russ. Joe Jessup here. I have good news for you."

Dodge instantly knew what this meant, and felt a quick rush of excitement. He said, "Old Fletcher's changed his mind."

"You got it."

Dodge took a drag on his cigarette, exhaled, and then said simply, "Wow."

"He's selling the whole enchilada."

Dodge took another pull on his cigarette. "Of all the sites I've looked at, the Peak is by far the best."

"By far, indeed. Now listen, the place isn't listed yet, so you've got a great shot at getting it. If you want me to, I'll put in an offer right now."

"Of course I want you to," Dodge said. "Offer the old guy twenty percent below what he's asking."

"Will do, but I'm sure he won't sell it for that."

"Just offer it to him and see what he says."

A few hours later, his telephone rang. Jessup had gotten a counter offer—ten percent below the asking price. "Jump on it," Dodge said.

"You're stealing it," Jessup said. "I'll fax you the papers as soon as I get them. You'll send me a binder."

He wired the money as soon as the papers arrived, ordered aerial photos and topographical maps, consulted his architect and engineer, and drew up a tentative plan.

A wide road would lead to the top of the mountain, and that's where the lodge would be built. It would have three hundred rooms, two indoor pools, an outdoor pool, a spa, a gym, a tavern and two restaurants. Tennis courts and an amusement park for kids would go out back. Nearby would go clusters of luxury condos for sale and for rent. The foot of the mountain, along Sheffield Road, would see an alpine village with twenty-five stores and restaurants: gift shops, a shop that sold skiing equipment, a health club, hair salon, art gallery. A championship golf course with breathtaking views and a state of the art clubhouse would pull people in from everywhere. Sheffield Peak would be a year-round destination—the hottest vacation spot in New England—not merely a ski resort.

Yesterday afternoon he had taken a plane from LaGuardia to Bangor, rented the nicest car in the lot, and driven two hours past snow-covered fields and evergreens to Darby, population 8,421 according to the sign he passed on the road. Once in his room at the Fireside Inn, a quaint little place in colonial style, the first thing he did was wipe slush off his oxblood loafers with one of the hotel's towels. After that—since people were so incompetent nowadays and couldn't be trusted—he called Jessup's office to check that the time and place of the closing hadn't been changed without someone letting him know. Nope: all was still set for eleven A.M. at the Safeguard Savings and Loan on Main Street, first floor, rear, room 106.

Anxious and tense, he went downstairs, sat at the bar, and ordered a dry martini. He looked at the rows of bottles in front of the mirrored wall and then at the windows. It was already black outside—at four thirty-five. It took a special kind of person to live in a place like this year round. The sun had sunk into the hills at ten of four.

The drink arrived and the very first sip of it burned his stomach. He asked for some water and swallowed a pill.

There were two other men at the bar, at its far end, talking about last Sunday's Patriots game. Dodge began thinking of

Tamarack in Vermont, his Jersey shore condos, his North Carolina mall. All nothing compared to what Sheffield Peak would become. He just couldn't wait to get his hands on that deed tomorrow. The best Christmas present ever!

Across the room, near the restaurant door, a Christmas tree twinkled with tiny lights. For some reason, it made him feel melancholy. This is a time of celebration, a time to rejoice, he told himself, but Christmas had never been one of his favorite holidays; there was always a sense of letdown connected with it, of dashed expectations. Tomorrow, however, there wouldn't be any letdown. Tomorrow he'd own the Peak!

He ordered another martini and sipped it slowly. Still feeling both sad and excited and wishing that Paula was with him, he went to the restaurant and ate alone: a steak with garlic mashed potatoes, salad, two glasses of pinot noir. He ordered a slice of strawberry cheesecake, but when it arrived he only took two bites. "Something the matter with your dessert?" asked the waitress, a sturdy young red haired woman. "Oh no, it's fine, I just ordered too much," Dodge said. The waitress took the plate away and soon returned with the bill. When he paid, he tipped her a little extra in the spirit of the season, then went outside to smoke.

The thermometer near the door said nine degrees and the sky was overcast. He shivered as he lit his cigarette. The lights in the inn's parking lot were shining on multiple mounds of plowed snow. No sweat about Christmas not being white in this neck of the woods, he just hoped that it wouldn't decide to get whiter tomorrow, while he was driving back to the airport.

His stomach gave him another quick jab as he suddenly thought: Suppose Fletcher changes his mind and the deal falls through? Blowing smoke at the frigid air he thought, Come on, don't be ridiculous. Why would he ever change his mind? There you go, at it again, always concerned about stuff that won't happen, one of your favorite tricks.

He stomped on the butt of his cigarette, then went to his room and swallowed another pill. He called Paula, but got her machine. Last minute Christmas shopping, he thought. But hey, I already have *my* gift. Almost.

His stomach angry, he watched TV until midnight, then fitfully slept.

It was still very cloudy and bitterly cold in the morning when Dodge started out for the Safeguard Savings and Loan. Occasional flurries, the TV weatherman had said. The guy better be right, Dodge thought; his plane would depart from Bangor at four twenty-five and he sure didn't want to miss it. Trying to get a flight tomorrow, Christmas Eve, would not be fun.

He arrived at the bank's meeting room a bit early, but Jessup and Jessup's lawyer were already there. The rep from the bank came in, and then Fletcher's lawyer, a thin old white-haired man named Osterfeld who wore a suit that looked like it dated back to the Hoover administration. He knew everybody but Dodge, and chatted them up while Dodge looked outside at the heavy clouds and tapped his pen on the tabletop. Finally the show got underway. The papers were all explained and signed and the bank handed over a check to Osterfeld. It was then that the old man said to Dodge, "Did anyone tell you that people are living out there?"

"On the mountain?" Dodge said with a sharp glance at Jessup. "No, nobody told me that."

"They caretake for Mr. Fletcher," Osterfeld said, "but don't own the land. I've already told them about the sale."

"They have houses there?"

"Well, more like camps."

Dodge wasn't exactly sure what the old dude meant by "camps," so he just said, "Oh."

Everyone smiled, shook hands, and went outside. On the bank's granite steps old Osterfeld scanned the sky with his watery eyes and said, "Well, looks like we're in for a big one."

"I sure hope not," Dodge grumbled. Then quickly he put on another smile and said goodbye to everyone and walked to his car with the precious deed in his hand.

He had been too excited to eat at the inn this morning, so now he decided to stop at the Darby Diner for Danish and coffee. Before he got back in the car, he took off his camel hair overcoat and his cashmere jacket and placed them across the back seat—he hated to be encumbered by outerwear when he drove—then quickly slipped behind the wheel and cranked up the heat to high. Man, it was *cold!*

The clouds had turned dark and ominous now, but still he decided to drive past his new acquisition. By using narrow Sheffield Road instead of Route 48, it would take him an hour longer to get to the airport, but he simply couldn't resist.

When the snow began falling, he tried not to be concerned, despite what Osterfeld had said. *It's just flurries*, he told himself. But all of a sudden the wind turned brisk and in no time at all he was in a real storm. How could that confident-looking, smiling weatherman have been so incredibly wrong?

So now here he was, still alone on the road with the snow coming down like mad. He wanted to pull to the side and stop, take a good long look at the land around here, but the shoulder was narrow and sloped toward a ditch, and what if a huge tractor trailer or logging truck came roaring down out of the snow and didn't see him sitting here until too late? He decided he'd better keep moving, and crept along, peering up at the mountain's hulking shape and wondering where those caretakers had their camps, shacks, whatever they were. He'd have to get someone to boot them out pronto—old Osterfeld?—but didn't see any buildings or lanes, just rocks and trees. *And I am the owner of every one of these rocks and trees,* he told himself, and felt a quick thrill.

He suddenly needed to talk to someone, and tried to call Paula again, to share his elation with her. Again he got nothing

but static. Making a sour face, he set the phone down on the passenger seat and scowled at the windshield. Where in the world was that old dirt lane? He hoped he hadn't passed it.

The road was now coated with snow and the sky was a fury of white against dark gray. He checked the dashboard clock again. He'd better quit messing around if he wanted to make his plane.

He gave the car a hit of gas and felt it fishtail a little. A nice big heavy sedan, but rear wheel drive, not good for snow. He touched the brake. The car gave a little shiver and felt unsteady.

He let out a breath and pressed on the pedal again, just gradually, slowly, and pictured that plane taking off without him. A little more gas—

And now he was facing a long steep grade with the road curving off to the left and he eased off the pedal again. Was *this* the hill where the access road lay? It looked kind of familiar to him.

There was still no one coming his way and no one behind him. Good deal, just take it nice and slow, he told himself, and started down the slope.

Then, without any warning, the wipers quit.

Instantly, the glass was covered, and Dodge could see nothing at all. A touch of panic hit and he rolled his window down, leaned forward and thrust his arm outside, attempting to grab a wiper, but the seat belt held him back. He clicked himself free and tried again. This time he managed to reach the wiper and give it a yank, but it didn't move. "Come on, you," he angrily shouted, "work!"

And then, to his horror, the car began sliding sideways down the hill. He pulled his hand back from the wiper and frantically turned the wheels toward the skid, but to no avail; the car kept sliding, faster, faster—and then all at once it was flying.

A frightening space of silence, of nothing at all, then an earsplitting jolt that shook his bones and the windshield was speeding straight at his eyes. He held up his hands but it struck him with blinding pain. Then all went black.

Chapter 2

Choose the land where you live with care.
Strive for clarity when you speak.
Keep an open mind when you govern.
When you deal with others, be kind.

—Tao Te Ching

"Just a little bit farther now," a man's voice said, and Dodge was aware of hands gripping his arms, strong hands, holding him up. He felt snow on his face, sharp cold, and remembered, *I wrecked the car,* and then he remembered more, a dream. A round face, staring dark eyes, the face of a little girl at the car's side window. *How did I get to China?*— that crazy thought—then he'd sunk into darkness again.

"You're doing fine," said the man. "Want to rest for a minute?"

When Dodge said yes, his voice was weak. His left thigh throbbed, and so did his head.

"How's your leg?" asked the man.

It was getting dark and the snow was thick, but Dodge could see the guy. He was wearing a black and green plaid jacket, a black woolen cap pulled over his ears. His chin and his cheeks were angular, and he looked to be past seventy. Dodge turned toward the other person who held him: a woman, about the same age as the man, almost as tall, and dressed in a similar way.

Dodge felt shaky and half awake. If these people let go of his arms, he would surely fall. His thoughts were confused and sluggish. Had somebody asked him a question? Maybe. "What?" he said.

"Your leg," the man said. "How's it feeling?"

"I hurt it," Dodge said. "My left one…my thigh."

"You told us that back in the car."

Dodge didn't remember this. The pain struck hard and he bared his teeth.

"Still pretty bad," the man said.

"Yeah."

"And how's your head?"

"My forehead hurts."

"You broke the windshield," the woman said.

"Can you see those lights up ahead?" asked the man.

"Just about," Dodge said. They were tiny and seemed to be swimming.

"That's where we live," the woman said. "Just a hundred feet more and we're there."

"Okay," Dodge said. He was shivering violently; this was the coldest he'd ever been in his life. He'd taken his jacket and coat off before starting out this afternoon, and only a thin dress shirt and an undershirt were keeping his skin from the elements.

"All set?" asked the man.

"All set," Dodge said.

"Here we go."

They were moving again. The snow was halfway up to their knees. Each step Dodge took drove agony through his thigh.

The man's breathing was labored and loud. He said, "How you doing, Doris?"

"Okay," said the woman. "How about you?"

"Not bad."

When they reached the porch the woman said, "All right now, up we go. Hold him tight now, Lee..."

"I got him," the man said.

They managed to navigate the steps and cross the porch. The woman opened the door and the two of them helped Dodge over the threshold.

Warmth instantly caressed his skin and he smelled something cooking. The fragrance was pleasant, but made him feel slightly ill. He saw a rectangular wooden table, a sink and a large black stove.

He was led through the kitchen and into the living room, then gently eased into a chair near a large stone fireplace. The fire burned merrily, throwing out plenty of heat. As soon as Dodge sat, a small dog, brown and white, came over and nudged his hand. "Charlotte, lie down," said the man, and the dog obeyed.

Dodge was lightheaded, shaking, and cold to his core. His heart was pounding.

"Lean back and relax now," the woman said, and she and the man left the room.

Dodge closed his eyes. Everything started to spin, so he opened them up again, holding the arms of the chair.

Now the woman was standing beside him. Her jacket and hat were gone; she was wearing a dark red sweater. Dodge looked at her pleasant, serious face, her short gray hair. She was sturdily built, rugged-looking. "It's time to take that wet shirt off," she said.

Dodge nodded, but couldn't do it; his hands weren't working right. He fumbled with the buttons helplessly.

"Let me," the woman said, and quickly unbuttoned the shirt and removed it. Dodge felt like a child, and hated it. "Now your undershirt, raise your arms." He did, the undershirt was gone, and the next thing he knew he was wearing a blue flannel shirt that the man had brought. The man said, "Let's do your feet," and slipped the oxblood loafers off then peeled off the thin black socks. "Your cuffs are a little wet, but they'll dry out soon."

The woman went to the sofa across the room, where a rust-colored cat was lying, and picked up a patchwork quilt. She draped it over Dodge as the man returned with a pair of wool socks and put them on Dodge's feet.

Dodge felt a sudden rush of warmth. His heart had slowed and his breathing was normal again. His leg was really killing him. His forehead didn't hurt too much anymore but now he had a headache. Another quick wave of giddiness struck, then passed. "You got anything for pain?" he asked. "Some aspirin or something?"

"Sure do," said the woman, and went to the kitchen again.

The kitchen, beyond a wide archway, was fairly bright, but the living room was dim, with pockets of shadow and dark. The man sat down in the chair on the opposite side of the hearth with the dog stretched out at his feet. Dodge didn't know what breed it was; he'd never owned a dog. He saw no point to it, unless you were blind or a hunter. He saw no point at all to owning a cat.

The pain in his leg rose up, and he gritted his teeth. When he looked at the sofa across the room, where the cat was lying, it seemed to jump. He squeezed his eyes shut hard, then opened them again.

Beyond the sofa, stairs on the far wall led into darkness. Dodge shifted his gaze to his left. Past the chair where the old man sat, a Christmas tree—or was it two?—stood in the shadows, undecorated. Dodge fought to make the images converge, then closed his eyes again. He'd seen another tree, a decorated tree, but where? Had he dreamed it? No, wasn't it in the bar—?

"We'll give it a minute to steep."

Dodge opened his eyes and the room spun around for a second. The woman was setting a steaming mug on the small end

table that stood on his right. "This tea will warm you up real quick," she said.

Dodge looked at the mug. Some *tea*. What he really could use was a good stiff drink. And where were the pain pills the woman had promised? He had some back in the car, in his jacket. His antidepressants were back there too. And a bottle of Scotch.

He watched vapor rise from the mug of tea. A wooden bird stood beside it. What kind of bird it was, and what kind of wood, Dodge didn't know. The carving was good, though, very accomplished. He did know a bit about art, thanks to his ex-wife, Jean, who used to drag him into galleries every chance she got in an effort to give him some culture.

"Your tea's almost ready," the woman said taking a seat on the sofa, "but not quite."

The man leaned forward, and firelight gleamed on his craggy, weatherworn face. "I guess we ought to introduce ourselves," he said. "My name's Lee Hansen, my wife's is Doris. What's yours?"

Dodge told him, then said, "I'm a lucky guy. If you hadn't found me…"

"You can thank our granddaughter for that," Lee said, and turned toward the Christmas tree.

Dodge looked at the tree. What he saw there gave him a jolt.

In the shadowy light stood the girl in his dream, the Chinese girl—not a dream after all. Was she standing there all along? If so, why hadn't he seen her? He thought he had seen two Christmas trees…

"Lee and I were inside," said Doris, "and Ruby was outside playing with Charlotte when she heard the crash. She ran in and told us, we all went to look, and there you were down in the gully with your windshield smashed. You were slumping forward, covered with snow, your seatbelt off and your forehead bleeding. You mumbled things we couldn't understand—something about an alpine village, it sounded like—and then you passed out. You probably don't remember."

"No," Dodge said.

"You woke up again and we asked where you hurt, and you told us your head and your leg. We sent Ruby back to mind the fireplace, and checked you out. We were sure that your leg wasn't broken, and managed to get you out of the car without much trouble. Broken leg or no broken leg, we couldn't leave you there, you'd have frozen to death."

"I guess." Dodge said, then frowned. "The driver's air bag didn't work."

"That's right," Lee said.

"No wipers and no air bag. Somebody's gonna pay. Big time."

"Your tea is ready now," Doris said. "You need any help with the mug?"

"I can handle it," Dodge said.

He lifted it with shaking hands and took a sip. The warmth felt good, but the taste was strange. "What kind of tea is this?" he asked.

"A blend of herbs mixed with raspberry honey," Doris said. "It will help your pain."

"You don't have any aspirin or something?"

"The medicine's in the tea."

How weird, Dodge said to himself, but took another swallow.

Doris and Lee and the girl kept watching him closely. Afraid he would faint again? He was sure that he wouldn't: the fire and quilt and tea were working wonders. He could see the child clearly now; his eyes had straightened out. She was small, maybe five or six, and stood perfectly still. There was only one Christmas tree, and the sofa was holding steady, cat and all. He was no longer cold, and was feeling much stronger. Even his troublesome stomach felt good. "That fireplace really does a job," he said. The one in his lodge at Tamarack gave little heat; it was mainly for show.

"It's a Russian design," Lee said. "The flue is constructed to capture gases with high efficiency. Emissions into the room are practically zero."

"Interesting," Dodge said.

"We use a tiny bit of LP gas and a lot of passive solar," Lee said, "but wood is our primary source of heat. We burn no oil at all. The way we see it, it doesn't make sense to go halfway around the world for fuel when the world's best fuel is right in your own back yard."

"Good point," Dodge said.

"Lee built that fireplace," Doris said.

"No kidding. That's pretty impressive."

"He built this whole place."

"With Doris's help," Lee said. "Without her I couldn't have done it."

"You're quite a team."

"We have a division of labor," Lee said. "I'm responsible for outdoor tasks and Doris is responsible for indoor tasks. I help her with her work and she helps me with mine."

Dodge smiled. He drank more tea and looked around again.

The room had a high cathedral ceiling with heavy beams, like the lodge at Tamarack. Colorful paintings and books lined the walls, which consisted of—what? Small triangular pieces of wood? On end tables flanking the sofa were more wooden sculptures of birds, and also some photos in frames: a smiling young couple in wedding clothes, and the Chinese girl.

Osterfeld said there were people out here in camps. This sure didn't look like a camp to Dodge. It wasn't luxurious by any means, but was built quite solidly, was very attractive, and unlike any house he'd ever seen before. All of its elements seemed to harmonize, to work together perfectly. "Nice looking place," he said, "but I don't understand what it's made of."

Lee laughed a little and said, "It's made of cordwood."

"You mean like the wood you burn?"

"That's right. But the house is made of poplar, and we don't burn poplar."

Dodge shook his head. "Incredible. And you and Doris built it."

"We did. We cut all the wood and did the construction work."

"Wow. How long did it take you?"

"Just under two years. It would've been less, but I messed up the first stretch of wall we built. I mixed the cement wrong and had to tear everything down and start over. Live and learn."

"It's beautiful," Dodge said. "And seems to hold the heat quite well."

"The walls are eighteen inches thick," Lee said. "Thus the deep windowsills. And eighteen inches of wood equals seven inches of fiberglass. That's pretty good insulation."

"It is indeed," Dodge said. He knew about insulation from his construction projects. "So who was your architect?"

Doris and Lee both smiled. "*We* were," Lee said.

"You didn't use an *architect?*"

"No, we knew what we wanted, so just went ahead and built it."

"'Cordwood Cottage,' that's what we call it," Doris said with a laugh.

"It turned out great," Dodge said. He took another sip of tea and Doris said, "You seem to be thinking clearly now."

"I'm back on the tracks," Dodge said.

The little girl stepped forward then, out of the shadows and into the flickering firelight. Her face was serious as she said, "There's blood on your head."

Doris said, "Yes, it's starting to weep again. Ruby, get me a wet cloth, please."

The girl went to the kitchen, ran water, returned with the cloth and gave it to Doris. She cleaned Dodge's forehead, then took the cloth back to the sink.

"It's not a big cut," said the girl.

"That's good to know," Dodge said.

"Your name is Mr. Dodge."

"It is, but you can call me Russ."

"Mr. Russ."

"Just Russ will do."

"I like Mr. Russ much better, it's politer."

Smiling, Dodge swallowed the last of his tea. "Okay, then," he said, "Mr. Russ it is. And you're Ruby, right?"

"Ruby Li Han-Sen."

"Nice name."

"My great-grandmother's name was Ruby and my Papa's name is Lee."

"Gotcha," Dodge said.

Ruby went to a metal box beside the fireplace, took out a log and carefully laid it on top of those that were burning. A flurry of sparks went up the chimney. She set the screen back in place and sat on the sofa next to Doris.

"Ruby's our fire girl," said Lee. "She makes sure we don't freeze."

"Papa cuts all the wood," Ruby said.

"But you, my dear, haul it inside."

"I do."

"And keep the fireplace going."

"Yes!"

"What would we do without you, Ruby?" Lee said, and the child laughed.

"How's your leg feeling?" Doris asked.

"Much better," Dodge said.

"Can you move it?"

He could. It was painful, but he could do it.

"Where does it hurt?"

"Right here." He laid his hand on it.

"You mind if I check it?" Doris said. "I was a nurse for thirty-five years."

"Be my guest."

He grimaced as she gently pressed his thigh from hip to knee. She said, "You've banged up your *rectus femoris.*"

"If you say so."

"Is your head feeling any better?"

"It is."

"You want more tea?"

"That would be good." He gave Doris the mug and she went to the kitchen again.

He checked his watch. It said four sixteen. His plane would take off in nine minutes. He said to Lee, "You mind if I use your phone? It's not going to cost you anything, I have a card."

"Sorry," Lee said, "but we don't have a phone."

Dodge couldn't believe it. "What? You live way out here in these woods and you don't have a phone?"

"No electric, either. Well, actually we do have a little solar power, mainly for our washing machine, but we're off the grid."

For the first time, Dodge realized: the light in the place was coming from sconces on the wall—that were fueled by gas? A kerosene lamp, unlighted, sat on the coffee table. Beside it was a fat yellow candle, also unlighted. What were these people, Amish or something? No, that couldn't be, they used electric, and Amish weren't allowed to do that, were they? Were they allowed to use gas? He didn't know. "I have a phone in my car," he said.

"Yes, we got it," Lee said, "but it doesn't work. Doris, bring in that phone, okay?"

Doris came back with the phone and the mug and set them down on the table next to Dodge. As she sat on the sofa again, Dodge tried the phone. It was totally dead. Terrific, he thought. No phone, and of course no e-mail. "Listen," he said, "there's someone I need to talk to, she's going to worry about me."

"I'm sure," Lee said. "But we really can't help you with that."

"There's nobody else around with a phone? I need to call someone to get my car back on the road."

"Only one other person lives in these parts," Lee said, "and he doesn't have a phone either. As for your car, I'm afraid it'll be a while before you'll be able to use it again. For one thing, it's stove in real bad. For another, the snow's too deep for someone to tow it."

Dodge frowned. He looked across the room to the Christmas tree. "Well listen," he said, "I appreciate what you've done for me, but I really can't stay here, I have urgent business to attend to."

"Locally?" Lee asked.

"In New York City."

"Oh, I see. Were you planning to fly?"

"Out of Bangor."

"The planes will be grounded tonight," Lee said, "and probably tomorrow, too. And who knows when the roads will be cleared, this looks like a monster storm. I guess your business will have to wait. I'm afraid we're stuck with each other. "

Dodge felt a cramp in his stomach. He pictured the people from Martin & Stern showing up at his office tomorrow and finding him absent. He always complained about the world's incompetence, and now the crew from Martin & Stern would think *he* was incompetent—or losing his memory. And so would his stalwart secretary, Julie.

Ruby was standing now with the dog at her feet and an eager look on her face. "Are you going to sleep here?" she asked.

"I'm afraid so."

"Good!" Ruby said. She jumped, and Charlotte barked.

Lee laughed. "It looks like somebody's pretty excited around this place," he said.

"Yes, me!" Ruby said. "And Charlotte, too!"

"We don't get much overnight company," Doris said.

"Uh-huh," Dodge said, thinking: Probably none. He looked at the child, and couldn't remember when, if ever, anyone had expressed such pleasure at his presence.

He felt a sudden pressure in his bladder; that tea, whatever it was, had gone right through him. "I'd, uh, like to use your bathroom," he said.

"Of course," Lee said. "You need any help getting out of that chair?"

"I don't think so," Dodge said. He attempted to stand, then winced and fell back.

"Let me give you a hand," Lee said.

He got Dodge onto his feet and kept holding his arm. "Slowly, now. Ruby, take his quilt off, please."

The little girl removed the wrap and watched intently as Dodge took a tentative step. Pain sliced through his leg and he felt a bit faint.

"You okay?" Lee asked.

Dodge nodded. The pain was bad, but the leg bore his weight.

Lee led him into the kitchen, past the sink—which was made of black stone of some kind, Dodge saw—past the black iron cook stove, which held a teakettle and pots. The little girl followed.

In front of the bathroom door, Lee said, "You think you can stand on your own?"

"Let's try it," Dodge said.

Lee let go of his arm.

"I can do it," Dodge said.

He went inside and closed the door, holding onto the latch to steady himself. When he turned, he saw a clawfoot tub, a pedestal sink, and a wooden box with a lid—the toilet. Good grief, it's a privy, he thought. A beautiful privy, adorned with carvings of fish and birds, but a privy all the same. After he used it, he washed his hands, and the water ran hot. The cake of soap was square and yellow; it looked homemade.

Under the single window, beside the sink, was a white rectangular box: a heating unit, fueled by gas. You could warm up this room real quick if you wanted to.

A wooden medicine cabinet was hanging above the sink. Dodge looked at himself in its mirror. The cut in his forehead was small and the bleeding had stopped—and so had the pain. That tea, whatever it was, had done the trick.

He opened the medicine cabinet's door. Its shelves held rows of small brown bottles with eyedropper caps. Hand-lettered labels

said tincture of this and that. He saw no pills of any kind. A larger bottle was labeled "Cough," another said "Fever" and Dodge thought: This Doris is one strange kind of a nurse. A witch doctor, maybe?

He looked in the sink cabinet drawers and found a couple of double-edge razors, some blades, some jars labeled "Cuts," "Bites," "Sunburn," "Rash." A syringe, a couple of new toothbrushes, a bottle of baby powder, petroleum jelly, a hairbrush, some combs and a pair of scissors. Barber's scissors? They probably cut each other's hair. A roll of flypaper.

Some paintings hung on the walls and he looked at them now. One was a lobster boat at sea, another a rowboat tied to a dock, the third a lake reflecting a mountain peak. Sheffield Peak? They were all very skillfully executed and had a mysterious tone that he found appealing. All were signed "Ellen Hansen." Wondering who that was, and how the bathroom water was heated, and what he had gotten into here, Dodge opened the door to the hall.

Chapter 3

Those who wish to control the world
cannot succeed.
Try to shape it and you'll destroy it.
Try to possess it and you'll lose it.

—Tao Te Ching

When Dodge left the bathroom, Lee was there waiting for him.

"My leg's okay," Dodge said. "I can walk by myself."

"Then let's walk to the table. You must be hungry."

"You better believe it," Dodge said.

When he'd come through the door of this house and smelled food he'd felt queasy, not even sure if he wanted to drink the tea that Doris had made, but now he was starving. All he had put in his stomach today, aside from the tea, was a coffee and Danish. So yes, he was dying to eat, but what would these people serve him? Raccoon stew? Squirrel pie?

35

As he entered the kitchen he thought of how quickly a life could change. A couple of hours ago he'd thought he'd be back in Manhattan tonight, dining at Dom's Trattoria, two blocks away from his condo. Instead he was going to eat with a couple of rustics out in the wilds of Maine. *My* wilds, he said to himself.

Lee pulled a chair out, the chair at the foot of the table, and said, "Here you go."

Careful not to bump his bad leg, Dodge sat as Ruby set out wooden bowls, ceramic cups, and silverware. For the first time, Dodge noticed the strings of onions and garlic that hung from the ceiling—and saw that the windows were covered now, with something that looked like thin quilts.

"If it's any consolation," Lee said, "you aren't the first one to go off the road at that spot. There ought to be a guardrail there, but the state says they can't afford it."

"Absurd," Dodge said.

"I agree, but that's what they tell us."

Shaking his head, Dodge muttered, "Government," then said, "A question for you. How do you heat your water, with gas?"

Lee shook his head. "Nope." He pointed. "You see that tank?"

It was copper, and stood in the corner. A number of copper pipes were connected to it and traveled across the wall to the cast iron kitchen stove. The effect was pleasing, like a piece of sculpture. "Oh, yeah, right," Dodge said. "But what do you do in the summer? You don't keep that stove going then, in hot weather, do you?"

"No, we switch over to solar," Lee said. "We have a collector outside."

Dodge nodded. "Clever," he said, thinking maybe a system like that, on a much grander scale, could be used in the lodge he would build—and maybe a Russian fireplace, too. "Who did you use to install this setup?"

"We did it ourselves," Lee said. "We did all of the work on this place ourselves."

Dodge said, "That's great," but was disappointed. He'd hoped to hear that a local contractor did the work, a firm he could hire for his massive project.

Doris brought over a platter of bread and a kettle of soup. This was what Dodge had smelled when he'd come through the door, stunned with cold.

Doris filled all of the bowls with soup as Ruby passed the bread. "Would you care for some grape juice, Mr. Dodge?" asked Lee, lifting a yellow pitcher.

"Call me Russ," Dodge said. "Sure, grape juice would be good." The grape juice called merlot or cabernet would be *really* good, but this would have to do.

Lee poured juice into everyone's cup. It was purple, but not real dark. Dodge took a sip, and hey, this was something special. It wasn't fermented, but it had *zing*. "This is great," he said. "The flavor is just so *fresh*."

"I make it in mid-September, when the grapes are at their peak," Doris said.

"You *make* it," Dodge said. "Do you grow the grapes?"

Lee laughed. "That's one thing I just can't grow," he said. Our neighbor, Clint, is the grape-growing champ, and he gives us some of his crop. This year it wasn't so great for some reason, but it was still plenty enough for four people."

Dodge drank again. "I love it. And the soup is delicious."

"I'm glad you think so," Doris said. "It's all home-grown. The tomatoes, the beans, the celery, the onions and garlic, even the spices. We have a wonderful garden plot. Over the years we've built up the soil, and now it gives us most of what we need."

"The bread is terrific too," Dodge said, "but I'm sure you don't grow your own wheat."

"No," Lee said, "we buy the wheat. But we grind it ourselves."

"*I* grind it," Ruby said.

"By hand?" Dodge said, remembering: no electricity.

"Yes."

"That must be hard."

"No, it's fun," Ruby said with a grin. "First I grind it coarse, then I grind it fine."

"Well it sure makes good bread," Dodge said, "really prime," and he thought of the stuff at Dom's. Tasty, but kind of like fluff compared to this. And Dom had never served a better soup. "How long you been living out here?" he asked.

"Twenty years," Lee said.

"We love it here," Doris said.

"But isn't it kind of lonely?"

"No, we don't find it so," Lee said. "We always have plenty to keep us busy, and Ruby to cheer us up."

Dodge thought: The granddaughter's not just visiting? She lives here all year round?

He had grown up next door to a boy whose parents had separated. The kid's mother had custody, but she was a tramp who drank a lot and palmed him off on her parents a lot of the time. Had something like that happened here? And was one of this child's parents Chinese? He wanted to ask these questions, but felt that it wasn't the time. Instead he asked, "How old are you, Ruby?"

"Six."

"You have any friends out here?"

"Charlotte's my friend, and Autumn, too."

"Autumn's your cat."

"Yes. We call her that because she came to us in the autumn. She was a stray."

"Uh-huh."

"And now she's a very good friend."

"I'm sure, but what about kids? Do you have any kids who are friends? "

"Yes, Sam," Ruby said. "He lives in Wilton Four Corners. And Elizabeth, too."

"We don't see them much in the winter," Doris said. "But they play at Todd Pond in the summer. That's out near Blackwood."

"Yes," Ruby said. "We swim and we play tee ball."

"Tee ball," Dodge said. "What's that?"

"It's like baseball, but nobody pitches. You hit the ball off this thing that sticks out of the ground. It's called a tee."

Dodge nodded, thinking about the golf course he planned to build on the mountaintop.

Ruby drank some of her grape juice then said to Dodge, "Do you know Alice in Wonderland?"

"I do."

"She had some funny friends."

"The White Rabbit," Dodge said. "The Mad Hatter."

"Yes!" Ruby laughed. "Will you read me that book tonight?"

Doris said, "I'm afraid our guest is too tired for that, sweetheart, but I'll read it to you."

Looking at Dodge again, Ruby said, "I can read books by myself, but I like it when people read to me."

"I liked that too when I was your age," Dodge said, and remembered teachers doing that, but not his parents. Since he didn't have kids himself or nephews or nieces, he'd never read books to children.

Ruby cleared the table and Doris brought tea—a different tea from the one Dodge had drunk before—and an apple dessert Dodge thought was great. "There's a flavor in here I can't pin down," he said.

"It's probably the maple syrup," Lee said. "We tap the trees in spring and we keep bees, too. Syrup and honey are our sweeteners."

"And we get beeswax," Ruby said.

"So tell Mr. Russ what we do with it, Ruby."

"Make candles and soap. I'll show you."

She ran off and quickly came back with the fat yellow candle that Dodge had seen in the living room. "I made this one," she said as she held it out.

"It's beautiful," Dodge said. "Good job. And that soap I saw in the bathroom—"

"Yes, that's beeswax too, and Mommom made it."

Dodge sat by the fire again as his hosts washed the dishes and Ruby helped put things away. He craved a cigarette—he always smoked one after meals—but they were back in the car. He saw no ashtrays in this place, so even if he had a cigarette they'd want him to smoke outside, which would be quite a feat in this storm.

Another thing he did after meals, and several times during the day, was watch the news, but the Hansens had no TV. They probably had a battery-powered radio, but he didn't see one anywhere. Without the news he felt grumpy, unsettled; his day was incomplete. And tonight he was itching to get a weather report, to learn when this storm was supposed to quit. Yeah, right, he thought—like weather reports are worth anything. Still, he wanted to hear one.

He scanned the room again. The paintings on the walls were mainly landscapes and very attractive: hills and fields and houses and boats on the water. All of them looked like the work of that same artist, Ellen Hansen. He looked at the colorful braided rug, at the afghan lying on the couch, and then at the long row of windows off to his right. Their thick deep shelf was filled with plants in various sizes of colored ceramic pots. The paintings and plants, along with the wall of books behind the couch, the sculptures of birds, the beams overhead, the fire with dozing cat and dog, had a pleasing, calming effect.

Dodge wondered what Paula was doing now. What would she think when he didn't appear tomorrow night—and didn't even call? Well, maybe the snow would stop pretty soon and he could get out of here tomorrow and catch a plane.

Lee entered the room and sat in the chair on the other side of the fireplace, then Doris and Ruby came in and sat down on the sofa. Doris began to read aloud from *Alice in Wonderland*, the chapter about the Queen of Hearts.

"I don't like the queen," said Ruby, "she's not nice. She hollers at people all the time and says she'll do bad things to them."

"Off with their heads!" Dodge said, thinking he'd said the equivalent on certain contentious occasions.

"Yes!" Ruby said.

The pain in Dodge's leg was only a soft throb now and the pain in his head had not returned. The food and the warmth of the fire had made him sleepy; as he listened to Doris read, he began to doze.

"Well, that's all for tonight," Doris said, and Dodge jerked awake. "Time to put your sleeper on."

Dodge checked his watch. It was only quarter of eight, but he was completely wiped out. As Ruby went up the stairs he said, "Lee, your toilet…it doesn't use water?"

"That's right, it's a composting toilet. We compost as much as we can around here, including our bodily wastes."

"You mean…the stuff that comes out of that toilet goes onto your garden?"

"Once it's been thoroughly composted, yes."

Dodge thought of the soup he had eaten. "But isn't that dangerous? To use human waste to grow food?"

"Bacteria destroy the pathogens, it's perfectly safe."

"You're sure."

"We've done it for twenty years without any problems," Doris said.

"That's interesting," Dodge said, hoping the string of trouble-free years would remain unbroken. "Who carved the sides of the toilet?"

Lee said, "I did. I love to carve."

"And these sculptures of birds, did you make them too?" He'd seen things like this at an auction once that went for a very good price.

"Yep, those are mine."

"Prime stuff," Dodge said as he stifled a yawn.

"You must be exhausted," Doris said. "Let me show you to your room."

Dodge didn't need any help getting out of the chair this time. Limping a little, he went through the kitchen and down the hall with Doris, thinking about his bottle of Scotch in the wrecked and buried car. He hated to miss his nightcap, but one thing these people didn't seem to make was moonshine—or even wine or beer.

They stopped at the door across from the bathroom. He'd noticed this room before. In the light from the hallway sconce, he saw a desk and chair, a bureau, a bed with a nightstand beside it. A kerosene lamp and a flashlight sat on the nightstand. Doris took matches out of the nightstand drawer and lit the lamp, adjusted the wick, and the room was aglow with soft light. "There's a robe on the back of the door," she said, "and something to wear to bed in the bureau. I've put your shirt and undershirt and socks in the washer across the hall. I'll be doing a wash tomorrow. You need anything at all, just let us know, and if you get hungry during the night, there's bread on the kitchen counter."

"Thanks." Dodge said. "And thanks for all your help."

"Don't mention it," Doris said. "Sleep as long as you want, and sleep well." She left him, closing the door.

In the bureau, Dodge found a pair of thermal underdrawers and a matching longsleeve shirt. Right out of Tobacco Road, he thought. All he needed now was a corncob pipe, and when summer arrived he could sit on the porch and tell tourists, "You can't get they-ah from he-ah."

He took off the stuff he was wearing, except for the socks, put the nightclothes on, then slipped into bed and turned off the kerosene lamp.

The sheets were cold and he shivered, thinking about how frozen he'd been when Doris and Lee had found him. These people, he thought, they don't know a thing about me—haven't even *asked* me anything about myself—and yet they take me in.

They're just so *trusting*. How do you get to be like that? I might be a crook on the run for all they know. I might be a serial killer.

The bed was warm now, comfortable, soft. The only sound was the wind outside, snow ticking against the window glass, and Dodge felt completely at ease, completely relaxed. He hadn't felt like this since—when? Maybe never, he thought. Maybe never.

Chapter 4

When the mud settles
the water becomes clear.
Can you restrain yourself
until this happens?

—Tao Te Ching

Dodge woke to dull gray morning light, and the room was utterly still.

The silence was broken first by a gust of snow at the windowpanes, then the voice of the little girl—in the kitchen, he thought. There wasn't any clock in the room, but he'd worn his watch to bed. It said 8:16.

As he pushed himself up, his leg reminded him of its injury, but the pain wasn't bad. When he sat on the edge of the mattress he felt a bit dizzy, and then he remembered he'd knocked his head. He stood up slowly and lowered his underdrawers.

The bruise on his thigh was a blue that was almost black, and stretched from hip to knee. Pulling the drawers back up again, he went to the window.

He rubbed at the moisture on the glass in order to see outside. The snow was still falling like mad, and how would he ever get out of this place? He thought of Paula back in Manhattan, wondering if she was worried because he hadn't phoned last night to say he was back in town.

He put on the robe that hung on the door and went to the hallway, holding his jockey shorts in his hand. The wonderful smell of something baking greeted him.

He opened the door to the right of the bathroom and entered a good-sized room with windows on the left-hand side and skylights covered with snow. He saw tools on the wall, a workbench, a potter's wheel, an empty clothesline, and one of those heaters he'd seen in the bathroom. He held his hand up to the heater; it was barely warm, but the room was far from cold.

Just past the heater was what he'd come in here for: the washing machine. He opened its lid and looked inside, and there, with a scramble of other clothes, were his undershirt, shirt, and socks. He tossed his jockey shorts in and closed the lid.

In the bathroom he used the toilet, once again intrigued by it, then went to the sink and looked in the medicine cabinet's mirror.

Wow! The lump on his forehead was purple and yellow and three inches wide. That had been *quite* a knock. He splashed some water on his face then dried it carefully, patting his forehead gently.

His toothbrush and razor and comb were back in his toilet kit, in the car. He remembered the stuff in the cabinet drawers, but decided he'd better not use any of it unless he asked. He rinsed his mouth, combed his hair with his hand. He'd be taking no antidepressant this morning, but figured it wouldn't hurt to skip a day.

Before leaving the bathroom he once again looked at the paintings that hung on its walls. Again, he was impressed.

《《——》》

46

Ruby and Lee were at the table and Doris was at the stove. They all said good morning, and Doris asked, "How did you sleep?"

"Like a log," Dodge said. "It's so *peaceful* here."

"And how are you feeling?"

"Much better."

"Your head's all purple!" Ruby said.

Dodge grinned. "And so is my leg, but I'm feeling good."

"I'm glad to hear that," Doris said, "but today you'll rest, you were pretty banged up."

"I think I'm okay," Dodge said, looking up at the windows. "I guess the plow didn't get here yet."

"We're caught in a blizzard," Lee said. "It'll be quite a while before we get plowed, I'm afraid. Probably tomorrow."

Dodge felt his heart sink and thought of Manhattan—of Paula, of Martin & Stern showing up at his office—then looked at his watch.

"Have a seat," Doris said. "We ate cereal early, it's our habit, but now we're having a second course in your honor. I made some muffins."

"Muffins," Dodge said. "My favorite." He sat, and Doris, wearing a yellow sweater today, came over and poured him some tea. Ruby gave him the basket of muffins.

A jar with something brown in it sat on the table. "What's this?" he asked.

"Apple butter," Lee said.

"Apple butter. No kidding. I haven't had any of that since I was a boy. You make it, Doris?"

Taking her seat now, Doris said, "I did."

"Doris can make almost anything," Lee said. "Anything to do with food, that is."

"We don't let Lee loose in the kitchen," Doris said, and laughed.

Lee also laughed. "I'm the world's worst cook," he said. "I tried my hand at pancakes once and they turned out like hockey pucks. But Doris, she's a whiz."

Dodge took a muffin out of the basket and broke it in half; warm mist escaped. He bit, he chewed, he swallowed and said, "This is the finest muffin I've ever tasted, Doris, I mean it is really *prime*." Dodge was a pretty accomplished liar, but this was no lie.

Again, Doris laughed. "Prime," she said. "First time anyone ever called my muffins *that*. They're just my regular plain old muffins, I didn't add any fruits or nuts, I didn't know if you'd like them."

"I like almost any kind of food," Dodge said.

"Try the other half with some apple butter," Lee said.

He did. "Fantastic," he said, "what flavor." He drank from his mug and said, "This tea is very…unique."

"A breakfast tea made out of herbs we grow," said Doris.

"I've never had anything like it before," Dodge said, and this, too, wasn't a lie: it tasted like a hayfield smelled on a hot summer afternoon—a nice enough smell, but not such a wonderful taste. Since he didn't want to offend, however, and coffee was not on the menu, he decided to drink it all. "You people are something," he said. "You said you grow most of your food."

"We do," Lee said. "We eat plenty of fruits and vegetables fresh in the summer, and Doris cans tons of stuff for the winter: raspberries, blackberries, peaches, applesauce, beets, tomatoes, green beans, chard... She makes cucumber pickles, tomato pickles and dilly beans. We dry beans and corn, and keep root crops down cellar—potatoes, turnips, parsnips, carrots. And cabbage, good old cabbage. We store a lot of apples, too, we have a small orchard." Looking at Doris he said, "Have I missed anything?"

"Onions and garlic," Ruby said.

"Good heavens, yes! Hanging right over my head and I forgot, I must be getting old."

"You're not!" Ruby said with a serious face. "You just forgot."

"Well, then, I guess I'll have to eat more rosemary, rosemary strengthens memory, and luckily we grow that too. And basil, thyme, oregano… It doesn't cost us much to eat, and we eat well."

"That's obvious," Dodge said. "Do you eat any meat?"

"We eat turkey on special occasions, thanks to Clint, who raises them, and also we eat a few fish. There's a trout stream here and Ruby and I do some fishing in spring and summer."

"I caught a brownie last year," Ruby said with a grin. "And Papa caught a rainbow and two brookies. He smoked the rainbow."

"We still have some left if you'd like to try it," Lee said.

"No thanks," Dodge said. "I'll stick with the muffins, I'm not a big fish man."

To say the least. He'd said that he liked most foods, which was true, but a major exception was fish. He *hated* fish. His father had worked in the office of a fish processing plant, and brought home tons of fish cakes, fish sticks, fish filets, fish nuggets— whatever the factory spewed out. By the time he was ten, Dodge was thoroughly sick of fish. The trout Lee smoked might be the world's greatest, but Dodge would never sample it, no way.

He broke apart another muffin and spread it with apple butter. These muffins really *were* the best—very substantial, not like those cupcakey things sold in stores.

"We grow plenty to sell at the farmers' market in summer," Doris said. "And plenty to give to the food bank to help the poor."

The poor, Dodge thought as he ate more muffin. The Hansens weren't exactly poor, but they sure weren't rich—yet they gave to others in need. Well, good for them, the world could use more people like that. "You grow peaches," he said. "I didn't think they'd survive in this climate."

"The right variety will," Lee said as he poured himself more tea. "But here's the thing. Our neighbor, Clint, has a terrible time with peaches—and I have a terrible time with grapes, which he grows incredibly well. We're only a few hundred feet apart, but the soil is different. My soil likes peaches and his likes grapes. Both of our homesteads have southern slopes, which is good for just about any crop, and boy, does it help us in winter. Once this blizzard quits, you'll see how sunlight floods the house. The stove and fireplace don't have to work very hard to keep us warm on bright days."

Dodge thought of his New York condo. The windows were on the north, which was great for an artist, but not for him, and he often turned on every light in the place to dispel the gloom.

He looked at the colorful grouping of landscape paintings beside the door and asked, "Did the same person paint all your pictures?"

"Yes," Doris said. "Our daughter-in-law."

"She's really good," Dodge said.

He'd been thinking that paintings like these were just what he needed to brighten up his condo. Maybe he could buy a few—and buy some for the ski resort and Tamarack while he was at it. "Does your daughter-in-law live nearby?" he asked.

"No," Doris said, "she doesn't."

Dodge wanted to follow up on this, but something in Doris's tone put him off. He remembered that kid from his childhood, the one whose parents had separated. But if Doris didn't like her daughter-in-law, would she cover the walls with her paintings? Maybe. People were funny.

"We're out of tea," Doris said, getting up. "I'll make some more."

"No more for me," Dodge said, "I've had plenty, and plenty to eat."

What he wanted now—what he really was *dying* for now—was a cigarette, but that was out of the question. He also wanted to hear the news; he really felt the lack of it. He said, "You don't have a radio, do you?"

"Sure do," Lee said. "Ruby, how 'bout you get it."

Ruby got up from the table, left the kitchen, and soon returned.

The radio was small and black. She held it tightly by its handle and rapidly worked a crank. "Okay," Lee said, "that's plenty, let Mr. Russ have it now."

Dodge took it and turned it on; he heard static, then something in…German?

"You have it on short wave!" Ruby said.

Dodge laughed. He pushed a switch and worked the tuning knob; got music, music, still more music, then finally the news. Ruby ignored it and helped clear the table.

A litany of world and domestic tragedies, the same old stuff as always, then the weather report. The snow would taper to flurries and end tonight.

Dodge felt a little embarrassed for having disrupted the peace. "Sure hope that forecast's right," he said.

"Me too," Lee said.

Dodge turned the radio off and set it down on the table. "Well now that I've eaten that wonderful breakfast," he said, "I'd like to get cleaned up. I didn't see a shower in your bathroom."

"No," Lee said, "we just have a tub."

Dodge smiled. "I haven't taken a bath in years."

"I hope you enjoy it."

"I'm sure I will. You wouldn't happen to have an extra toothbrush, would you?"

"Of course," Lee said. "There are some in the bathroom cabinet, second drawer down, and a jar of tooth powder too. You'll also find a comb and a razor, along with the shaving soap and brush."

Again Dodge smiled, thinking, *Soap and brush. An interesting experience awaits.* "I'll be a new man," he said, and Ruby laughed.

Chapter 5

Clear your mind: embrace emptiness.
Let your heart be tranquil
as you watch the tumult of things
return to the source.

—Tao Te Ching

The tub was deep and the water was soothing and made his whole body feel better, but man, did his leg look ugly. He knew he was very lucky it hadn't been broken. He was lucky to be alive!

On the edge of the tub, beside the wall, were a couple of small, unpainted wooden ships. Lee's handiwork, Dodge assumed. He picked one up and examined it. Its doors and portholes and decking—all its details—were exquisite. He thought of what patience it took to make a thing like this, what attention, what care. He'd never be able to do it. Patience had never been one of his strong suits, to put it mildly.

He set the boat down on the water; its balance was perfect. He thought of Ruby playing with this, what fun she must have. He thought of her serious face and her smiling face. His ex-wife, Jean, had wanted kids, but he'd said no. Kids ate up your time, not to mention your money. They didn't fit into his plans.

He gave the boat a little push, remembering playing with bathtub toys when he was a kid, a million years ago. As the boat skimmed over the water, quick and true, he thought with a smile: If Paula could see me now.

He looked at the composting toilet, its intricate carvings, and then at the lobster boat painting. Nice setup these people have, he thought, their own little world. The problem is, it isn't the *real* world.

He rinsed himself off and toweled himself dry, then went to the sink and took out a toothbrush, the jar of powder, a comb, and the shaving soap and brush. After combing his hair, careful to avoid that nasty bump on his forehead, he brushed his teeth. The powder tasted like cinnamon.

Now for the shave. He wet the brush and swirled it across the bar of honey-colored soap; it lathered right up and worked just fine, better than the canned foam he was used to.

In the bedroom he put the knitted underwear back on, and then his slacks; their cuffs were totally dry. He put on the blue flannel shirt and wool socks, made the bed, then went to the kitchen.

Ruby was at the table with Doris, but Lee wasn't there. Doris inspected a paper the child was working on, and said, "Good job."

Dodge could see the paper now: it was filled with addition problems. "Snow day," he said. "No school."

"This is my school," Ruby said, using her serious face. "My Mommom and Papa are my teachers."

"But don't you go to another school too?"

"No, just this school. Maybe next year I'll go to another one—on the bus."

"I see," Dodge said with a nod.

Looking at him, Doris said, "You're walking better, Mr. Dodge."

"That soak in the tub really helped, and so did last night's tea. Now please, no more of this 'Mr. Dodge' stuff, call me Russ."

"Russ," Doris said.

Dodge smiled. "Good." Then he looked at the large array of south-facing windows and frowned, "No letup."

"I love big snows!" Ruby said.

"I used to love them too when I was a kid," Dodge said. "School was called off and I used to go sledding."

Turning to Doris, Ruby said, "Can I go sliding, Mommom?"

"Maybe later," Doris said. "It depends on how windy it is."

Dodge looked at the windows again and said, "How much land do you own here, if you don't mind my asking?"

"None," Doris said.

"You built this house on land you don't own?"

"That's right. We caretake the land for the owner, who lets us live here."

Dodge nodded. This is what that lawyer, Osterfeld, had said. A few people lived on Fletcher's land, but didn't own any of it.

"Am I finished now, Mommom?" Ruby asked, holding her paper up.

"You are, and you did your usual excellent job."

"When will we make the cookies?"

"When Papa gets back," said Doris, and looked at Dodge. "We make cookies to hang on the Christmas tree."

"And popcorn!" Ruby chimed in.

Dodge smiled. "That sounds like a lot of fun."

"Christmas is one of my favorite holidays," Ruby said. "And New Year's and Children's Day and Moon Festival, too."

"Children's Day and Moon Festival?" Dodge said. "I don't know those holidays."

"They're Chinese holidays."

"Oh, sure."

"And sometimes we make moon cakes."

"No kidding? Are they made out of pieces of moon?"

"Of course not!" Ruby said, laughing. "They're made out of rice flour."

"Rice flour. Must be good."

"They're delicious! When will we make them, Mommom?"

"On Chinese New Year's."

"Is that a long time?"

"Pretty long. But today we'll make cookies."

"Soon?"

"Pretty soon. Now why don't you put on your jacket and go to the porch and see if Papa's coming. But don't leave the porch."

"I won't," Ruby said.

She went to the coat rack and took down her jacket and slipped it on.

"And your hat," Doris said.

Ruby put that on too and went out the door. A cold gust entered the room as she closed it behind her.

"Lee went to check on our neighbor," Doris said. "And while he's out, he'll look at your car. I didn't want him to go alone, but as usual he wouldn't listen. He lost a lung in the service years ago, in combat, when he was a medic, and sometimes he gets pretty winded. I hate to see him go out by himself in this kind of weather, but he always says not to worry."

The door came open again and Ruby ran in excitedly. "Papa's coming!" she said.

"Well, that's a relief," Doris said.

A few minutes later Lee came through the door, stamping his feet and holding a burlap bag. "The storm's just as strong as ever," he said.

Doris took the bag from him. "How's Clint?"

"Doing fine. His place is warm as toast and he had a big oatmeal breakfast."

"Thank heavens," Doris said, and then, to Dodge: "Clint Ferguson's lived on Sheffield Peak for over thirty years. He helped us a lot when we first came. He's ninety-three and still grows his own food and still cuts all his wood by hand."

Dodge raised his eyebrows. "Quite a guy."

"We keep tabs on him," Doris said. "He's a little forgetful at times."

"We don't want him wandering out in this weather," Lee said.

"I don't want *you* wandering out in this weather," Doris said, and Lee laughed.

"So you looked at my car?" Dodge asked.

"Well, I tried to," Lee said, "but it's buried, completely covered. You'd never even know it was there."

Dodge shook his head. "Oh, great."

"We're going to make some Christmas cookies, Papa," Ruby said.

"That's wonderful," Lee said. "It's one of my favorite things to do."

Doris looked in the burlap bag. "The bird's a beauty, and clean as a whistle, as always. If there's one thing I really hate to do, it's clean chickens and turkeys."

"Can I see it?" asked Ruby.

Doris lowered the bag. "It's big!" Ruby said as she peered inside, then she frowned. "Are whistles clean, Mommom?"

"They better be, if you want a nice clear sound."

"The whistle Papa carved for me is *loud*. It must be *very* clean."

"And you must have very strong lungs," said Doris, putting the bird in the fridge.

"I do!" Ruby said.

Lee took his hat and jacket off and hung them in the entryway, then sat at the table. Dodge's leg was acting up a bit, so he sat too. Lee said to him, "Clint raises some turkeys and gives us a bird for Thanksgiving and Christmas, then comes to our house for dinner. But if this storm won't quit, the dinner may have to go to *him* this Christmas day."

"Lee, you look frozen," Doris said. "You need more tea to warm you up."

"I'd love some, darling."

"Russ?"

"No thanks," Dodge said. "I'm fine."

As Doris took the teapot from the stove and filled Lee's cup with steaming water, Dodge checked his watch again. It said 10:06. The team from Martin and Stern was probably at his office now, receiving the news that nobody knew where he was. He felt a sharp jab in his stomach.

"How 'bout we make those cookies now, Ruby," Doris said.

Ruby's eyes widened. "Yes!"

She went to a cabinet beside the sink, leaned down, and took out a yellow canister. Then she climbed on a stool and opened an upper cabinet door and brought out baking powder, salt, vanilla and a jar of maple sugar. Doris took milk and eggs and butter from the fridge.

When all the ingredients were on the counter, Ruby set to work with Doris' help. "Two and a half cups of flour," Doris said, and Ruby dipped the metal cup inside the canister. "Two teaspoons of baking powder…"

And so it went. With an eggbeater, Ruby beat the melted butter and sugar and eggs and milk and vanilla together. She took a turn mixing the dough with a wooden spoon.

While this project advanced, Dodge said to Lee, "Those toy boats in the bathroom—you made them, I guess."

Lee nodded. "You guess right."

"And he made the chair you're sitting on," Doris said. "And all the other chairs, of course, and the table."

"I just love working with wood," Lee said.

"Well, you sure are good at it," Dodge said.

The dough was ready. Doris rolled a batch of it out on a

wooden cutting board—which Lee had also made—then took the board to the table. She brought out some baking sheets and cookie cutters. "Can I go first?" Ruby asked.

"Maybe our guest would like to go first," Doris said as she buttered a baking sheet.

Dodge said, "Oh, no, let Ruby go first."

"Thank you," said Ruby, and picked up a cutter shaped like a star. With care and precision, she cut out the cookie. "Good job," Lee said. Ruby did one of each of the three other shapes: a bell, a Christmas tree, and the head of Santa Claus. "Now it's your turn," she said to Dodge.

Dodge felt a bit anxious. He'd never made cookies. His *mother* had never made cookies. He laughed as he picked up the star-shaped cutter. "I'm new at this," he said. "Well, let's see what happens."

He pressed the cutter into the dough. It stuck a little, and one of the points of the star came out missing its tip. "Darn," he said.

"That's the hardest one to do," Ruby said. "Try the bell, it's easier."

It was, and turned out perfectly. Dodge did a Santa and tree, then Lee took over. They kept taking turns until all of the baking sheets were full.

Dodge looked at his watch again, thinking, *I should be deep in a meeting now, and what am I doing? Making a batch of cookies out in the boonies.* He'd planned to phone the manager of his mall about a prospective tenant after the morning's meeting ended. Time was flowing, opportunities were being missed, and work was piling up. He'd have a zillion calls and e-mails to answer when he got back. He let out a breath and looked—once again—at the window. The snow was relentless. He said, "You get many storms this big?"

"Just a couple a year," Lee said. "But it snows nearly every week, so the ground's always covered."

Good news, Dodge thought. He'd install snowmaking machines, of course, but with luck he wouldn't have to use them much.

Ruby put on her jacket, then went through the hallway and out the back door. Soon she returned with a canvas sling filled with firewood. She opened the metal box near the kitchen stove and dumped it in, then went outside again.

"Quite the worker," Dodge said.

"She's a wonder," Lee said. "She wants to help with everything—and she does. She brings in all the wood, tends the fireplace, helps Doris cook…"

"Amazing kid," Dodge said.

Feeling restless now that the cookie-making job was finished—man, did he need a cigarette!—and thinking about his office again, he went to the paintings beside the door and examined them closely.

The one he liked best showed a dark sloping roof and a high dark treetop pressing against a pale yellow evening sky. It was ominous in a way, and yet, at the same time, uplifting. Later on, when the time seemed right, he'd ask where—or if—he could buy some of Ellen's work.

He wandered into the living room and looked at the books on the shelves in there. Lots of them had to do with nature: *Trees of North America*, *Birds of North America*, etc. There were plenty of books on building, of course: *Modern Carpentry*, *Essentials of Plumbing*, *Energy from the Sun*, *The Straw Bale House*. Making a house out of cordwood was one thing, Dodge thought, but straw? It sounded like something that one of the three little pigs would do.

Aside from all the practical stuff, there were rows of classics: Montaigne, Marcus Aurelius, Emerson, Thoreau… Dodge wondered if the Hansens actually read this stuff. A paper was pinned to a lower shelf. It said: "Not one is demented with the mania of owning things." One what? Dodge wondered. And…demented? Mania? Wasn't that just a little bit over the top?

Ruby came back inside again, this time with bigger wood, which she placed in the box near the living room hearth. She threw a stick into the fireplace and jabbed at it with the poker. "There," she said, replacing the screen, then went to Dodge, whose attention had now been caught by a small model house that sat on the shelf below the living room's windows.

"That's our cottage," Ruby said. She pointed to a cylinder against its wall. "This is the solar hot water collector. Papa told you about it."

"He did indeed. He made this little house, of course."

"Of course."

"It's wonderful."

"Yes," Ruby said, "but you should see the dollhouse he made, it's not little, it's *big*. You want to?"

"Sure," Dodge said.

"Then come with me!"

Chapter 6

Great intelligence seems foolish.
Great eloquence seems hesitant.
Great achievement seems flawed.

—Tao Te Ching

Ruby ran across the room and started up the stairs. Dodge followed her, holding the railing. His leg protested at every step, but the pain wasn't really bad.

Ruby's bedroom was filled with delights: luminous stars spread a firmament over the ceiling, a kite in the shape of a dragonfly hung near a window, and tall shelves were stacked with stuffed animals, books and toys. Many of the toys were made of wood, like the boats in the bathtub.

The dollhouse sat at the end of the bed—the most fabulous dollhouse Dodge had ever seen. Not that he'd seen a lot of them, but he remembered marveling over one in some crafts museum that Jean had steered him into, and this was at least its equal.

It looked to be four feet wide by three feet tall. Its outer walls were covered with clapboard, painted white, and its roof was slate. The chimneys, one at the end of the house and one in the center, appeared to be made of real brick.

"What a beautiful house," Dodge said. "Do you mind if I touch it?"

Ruby smiled. "No, I don't mind."

He touched the roof—and the "slate" was actually wood. He touched a chimney. Wood. "Incredible," he said.

"I love it," Ruby said with a grin. "I play with it every day."

Dodge looked at the dollhouse kitchen: the sink, refrigerator, stove, the beadboard cupboards, table, chairs—all made of wood. Some of the items were painted and some were plain. The bathroom had a toilet, sink, and tub—with a shower. "Mommom made the shower curtain," Ruby said.

The curtain hung on tiny rings, and Dodge moved it back and forth with his finger. "Neat," he said.

The dining room was empty—had no furnishings at all—and the living room held just a couch and two easy chairs.

"Papa carved the chairs and couch, then Mommom covered them," Ruby said. "I need more furniture." She lowered her voice to a whisper and said, "I think I'm getting more for Christmas."

"Ah-hah," Dodge said.

On the upper floor, another bathroom—with only a pedestal sink so far—and four bedrooms. Just two of the rooms had beds. On one of these beds sat a little girl, and a bed in another room had an older couple lying on it. In the room at the end of the hallway, a young couple sat on the floor.

"Let me tell you about my house," Ruby said. "The girl on the bed is Amy. She came from China when she was a baby. China is very far away. Amy wants to go there when she's big because she can't remember anything about it. Amy's Mommom made the quilt that's on her bed. She made the pillows, too, and the window curtains, and she made the rug."

Ruby shifted her gaze to the room next door. "That's her Mommom and Papa on the bed. They work very hard and go to bed early. They'd like to go to China too, but it costs too much. But they read Amy books about China."

Ruby now looked at the room at the end of the hallway. "That's Amy's Mommy and Daddy," she said. "They don't have a bed, so they sleep on the floor!" She laughed. "They're asking Santa for a bed."

"I bet he'll bring them one," Dodge said. "And what are you asking Santa for?"

Ruby frowned for a moment, her lips compressed. Her eyes took on a distant look. She said, "I'm asking him to let my Papa and Mommom live for a thousand years."

This reply was totally unexpected, and startled Dodge. Why would a child say such a thing? He said, "That's a very long time."

"Yes, it is," Ruby said, and her voice was soft. Then, turning away from the dollhouse, she looked at the ceiling. "You like my dragonfly?"

"It's beautiful."

"It came from China."

"I thought so."

"It's a kite, and it really flies. When springtime comes I'll fly it with Papa. I did it last springtime."

"That must be a lot of fun."

"It is, but sometimes the wind is so strong that it almost pulls it out of my hands. Then Papa helps me. If I let it go, it might fly all the way back to China!"

Dodge laughed, then Doris's voice came up the stairs. "It's time to decorate the cookies. Anyone want to help?"

"Me!" Ruby said, and ran to the hallway. "Come on, Mr. Russ!"

Some cookies sat on a tray on the kitchen table, and next to the tray were a platter, some small paintbrushes, cups with colored liquids in them and a jar of water.

"Everyone gets six cookies to decorate," Doris said. "We'll hang those on the tree. The rest we'll leave plain and eat."

"These cookies are really good," Ruby said.

"Oh? How do you know?" Lee said. "You didn't eat any yet."

"We made them before, last year. But Mommom burned the second tray, remember?"

Laughing, Doris said, "I certainly do. I was wool-gathering here at the table, and next thing I knew, I smelled smoke."

"What's 'wool-gathering' mean?" Ruby asked.

"It means lost in a daydream," Doris said. "You know what a daydream is."

"I do, I have them sometimes. I like them."

"Me too," Doris said, "but they're not good to have when you're cooking. We used those ruined cookies on the tree, and you know what I think? I think we should all eat one of this year's batch right now to see if they turned out well."

"So do I!" Ruby said, and eagerly took one, a Santa, and bit off his cap. "It's good!" she said. "Not burnt at all!"

"Russ, are you going to try one?" Doris asked.

"Of course."

He picked one up, a bell, and took a bite, and suddenly remembered: his father's mother, grandma Dodge, had made cookies like this, with a texture and depth of flavor no bakery could hope to duplicate. "Ruby, you're right," he said, "they *are* good—delicious—and *you* helped make them. Maybe you'll be a cook when you grow up."

"No," Ruby said with her serious look. "I'm going to be a doctor."

Dodge raised his eyebrows. "A doctor," he said. "Well, good for you."

"I want to help people be alive."

"For a thousand years?"

"That's right."

The cat crossed the floor and jumped to the windowsill. Doris was smiling, but something was sad in her smile. "Well, let's get busy here," she said.

Dodge was entranced by how carefully Ruby worked; by the pains she took to not let the colors run into each other. Her attention was totally focused on her task. His own attempts were merely passable. Of course, he hadn't painted anything since grammar school.

He said, "These dyes smell really good."

"I made them out of plants," Doris said.

"No kidding. What's this red one made out of, strawberries?"

"You have an excellent nose."

When the cookies were finished, Doris said, "Now don't these look just beautiful. We'll let them dry real good, and tonight they'll go on the tree."

"I can't wait!" Ruby said.

For lunch they had more of the soup they had eaten the night before, with more of the bread. When the meal was over, Ruby said, "Papa, can we go sliding?"

"Well, let's take a look," Lee said. He went to the door and opened it up, paused for a moment, then said, "I think we should give it a shot."

"Yes!" Ruby said, and jumped. "Can you come with us, Mr. Russ? Papa can give you a coat—"

"I think Mr. Russ would probably like to stay inside," Doris said. "Remember, he hurt his leg."

"It feels okay right now," Dodge said. "And actually, I'd like to go outside and watch for a little while."

"Good!" Ruby said.

After she helped clear the table, Ruby donned a hooded purple snowsuit, mittens and boots. Lee gave Dodge some winter wear: a jacket, wool pants that he couldn't zip up all the way and ended at his ankles, mittens (he hadn't worn mittens since grammar school), a hat and a pair of boots. The three of them went through the door, followed by Charlotte. On the porch, Lee grabbed a shovel and cleared the steps.

Charlotte bounded ahead, the fluffy light snow nearly up to her neck, closely followed by Ruby, pulling her sled. The sled was an old-fashioned wooden kind, but looked quite new to Dodge. "My Papa made this sled," she said, her voice sounding small in the snow and wind. "Do you like it?"

"I love it," Dodge said. "It's prime."

Ruby laughed.

Snow rapidly coated the sleeves of the jacket that Dodge was wearing. He turned and looked back at the cottage, his face all wet, and there was the solar hot water collector, capped with snow. The roof was also covered with snow, and he couldn't make out the solar panels or skylights.

He laughed to himself. Going outside in snowstorms wasn't his cup of tea, yet here he was. He had never gone skiing and probably never would, even at his own resort. When he went on a skiing trip with Paula he sat around in the lodge with a drink and some magazines while she hit the trails. She'd be stunned to see him wading through knee-deep drifts—and liking it!

They walked toward a stand of barren trees that were all the same size and evenly spaced. The orchard, Dodge realized, and this was the southern slope that Lee had talked about. Lee started to shovel. "Snow's too deep for good sliding," he said.

He shoveled a path down the slope, and soon his breath was coming hard. Dodge remembered what Doris had said about Lee's lung, and after a couple of minutes he said, "Can I take a turn at that?"

"You sure you want to, with that leg of yours?"

"I'm sure," Dodge said.

He took the shovel from Lee and set to work, and soon he too was breathing heavily; he was more out of shape than he'd thought. He knew he should go to his fitness club more frequently, but it was hard to find the time. He should lose some

weight and stop smoking, too, his cough had been chronic for several years. But he hadn't done very much coughing here; in this mountain air, his lungs felt good. Maybe the break from cigarettes he was having would help him quit.

After the shoveling was complete, the three of them trudged up the path they had made, packing the dry snow under their feet. When they reached the top, Ruby said, "Mr. Russ! Watch me slide!" and she jumped on her sled and took off, followed by running Charlotte.

Dodge smiled. "Slide," he said.

"Yes, that's what we call it in Maine," Lee said. "In other places, kids go sledding, or maybe coasting, but here they go sliding."

Ruby came back up the hill, dragging the sled behind her, her cheeks red with cold. Charlotte stood next to her, panting.

"Great slide," Dodge said.

"This time I'll go even faster," Ruby said, and flopped on the sled again.

As he watched her go speeding along, Dodge saw an image of skiers in his mind. He pictured the brand new access road. It had to replace the existing road, no other place was suitable— which meant it would practically go through the Hansens' house.

Well, houses could be moved. If Cordwood Cottage was relocated a hundred yards off to the east…

He caught himself. What? What was he thinking? The Hansens could *stay* here?

He saw Ruby come to a stop down below, the dog running happily past her, and thought: Well, hold on a second, was that such a crazy idea? He would need a large maintenance crew. Maybe Doris and Lee could be part of that crew and live onsite. They knew this land better than anyone else…

But what if they didn't accept that plan? In that case he'd help them to find a new home, what else could he do? What a shame that it had to be decent, hardworking people like them who lived on this mountain instead of some outlaw moonshiners.

Ruby came slogging up the hill. When she reached the top, Charlotte ran over to Dodge and nudged his knee.

Dodge stroked the animal's head and Ruby said, "She loves you!"

"You think so?" Dodge said with a smile.

"She does! And she wants you to slide!"

"It looks like great fun, but I'm way too big for your sled."

"Oh," Ruby said with a frown. Then, brightly, "Well come on, Charlotte, let's go!"

What a time she was having, and Dodge remembered: when he was Ruby's age he'd played with other kids much more than Ruby did—primarily war and cowboy games—but he'd also spent hours in front of the TV set, hungering for the stuff it was selling, something that Ruby didn't do. And back in those distant days, when he watched those shows, he used to think: When I grow up I'll make enough money to buy anything I want. *Everything* I want.

As he watched Ruby start up the hill again he suddenly thought of that quote he had seen in the living room... *the mania of owning things*. At this point in her life, Ruby seemed pretty immune to that.

Again and again, Ruby sped down the slope. Each time she came back up with happy Charlotte at her heels she made an excited, delighted comment. "I almost fell off!" "Snow hit my face!" Dodge laughed, but the cold and exercise had set his thigh to throbbing again and he said to Lee, "I'm heading back, my leg doesn't like it here."

"Sure, sure, go on," Lee said. "We're not going to stay much longer ourselves."

Chapter 7

When the rich become ever richer
while granaries are empty;
when governments squander treasure
on armies instead of inventions;
when the privileged live in luxury
while those in need despair:
chaos will rule the land.

—Tao Te Ching

*B*ack in the cottage, Dodge changed his clothes in the bedroom then stood by the kitchen stove to warm up. Doris
was at the table, busily knitting something purple, her nee-
dles steadily clicking. She said, "You have a good time out there?"

"I had a terrific time," Dodge said. Then, raising his eyebrows: "What smells so good?"

Doris smiled, intent on her knitting. "My special Christmas cake," she said. "I make it every year."

"It smells fantastic."

Without looking up, Doris said, "We eat it on Christmas night. With luck, you'll be on the road by then, but I'll make sure you get some."

With luck, Dodge thought, and felt a tight pinch in his stomach. His leg started hurting again and he sat down across from Doris. "I'm starting to think it'll never stop snowing," he said.

"Oh, it's a real jeezer, all right," Doris said.

Dodge grinned. "A real jeezer. I don't know that expression."

"I guess it's unique to Maine. You're not from Maine."

"No, I'm from Manhattan."

"You're here on vacation?"

Dodge hesitated a second, then said, "That's right, I went skiing."

"At Shoehorn, I guess, that's the only resort near here."

"Yes, Shoehorn."

"And what kind of work do you do in Manhattan?"

"I'm in advertising."

"You make commercials?"

"No, print ads," Dodge said. "For banks and clothing stores, places like that."

The lies were rapidly piling up; he figured he'd better switch topics. "Ruby is having a wonderful time in the snow," he said. "She's so full of life."

"She knows that life is for *living*," Doris said. "Luckily, Lee and I are retired and have the time to give her lots of memories."

An interesting way of looking at things, Dodge thought. Suddenly the questions he'd wanted to ask for quite some time became urgent. Frowning, he said, "When she showed me her dollhouse she said some things...some things that made me wonder about her parents."

"Her parents were killed in an auto accident three years ago," Doris said. She stopped knitting and looked at her hands.

Dodge caught his breath. "How horrible," he said.

Without looking up, Doris said, "They lived in a nice apartment in Blackwood, and Lee and I were babysitting there the night that the accident happened. Jeff was a social worker at Helping Hands, an agency in town. One of his colleagues had taken another job, and there was a farewell dinner for him. Jeff picked Ellen up at Blackwood High, where she taught art, and the two of them went to the dinner together. Afterwards, they were driving back to the school's parking lot, where Ellen had left her car, and a man in a pickup hit them head on and killed them both. He was drunk."

"My God," Dodge said.

Doris lifted her head and looked out at the gray, blank windows. "If only I could forget," she said. "Forget it all, but especially that time when we had to tell Ruby. She couldn't really understand, of course, she was only three, but the way she kept crying, it broke our hearts."

Dodge said nothing, just nodded.

"My son was an only child," Doris said. "And so was Ellen. Her parents had died some years ago, so we were the only living kin, and became Ruby's guardians. We love her with all our hearts, and she loves us, but to not have your mother and father…"

She stopped. Her mouth was quivering. "And losing your only child," she said, "and our wonderful daughter-in-law… Both of them gone forever, just like that…"

"I can't imagine," Dodge said.

Doris looked down at her knitting again. She said, "Jeff and Ellen had tried for eight years to have children, without success. They had taken a trip to China once, and decided to try to adopt a Chinese baby. The process took over two years. When the agency told them about little Ruby, they were ecstatic…and so were we. A grandchild! And when they came back from China with her, Lee and I felt such joy.

"We loved her from the moment we first set eyes on her. The

first time I held her in my arms—I will never forget it, ever. This little flower, fourteen months old, abandoned on the steps of a lumberyard as an infant, wrapped in a thin red blanket with the date of her birth pinned to it. Delivered by the police to an orphanage, lucky enough to be taken into a wonderful, loving home. Everything going so well, and then, to have this happen…"

Tears suddenly flooded her eyes. "Forgive me," she said.

Dodge felt suddenly heartsick. For a moment he couldn't speak. Then he said, "But you and Lee…Ruby's still in a wonderful home."

Wiping her eyes with her fingers, Doris said, "We love her with all our hearts. But we're old. We do our best, and we hope to live till she's in her teens, but at our age you never know what will happen."

The house was quiet, except for a slight hissing sound from the stove. Doris let out a breath and said, "That dollhouse you saw upstairs is a copy of our old house, the house in Darby where Lee and I raised Jeff. It doesn't exist anymore, the state tore it down for a highway. Did you ever take Route 48?"

"That's the road I came in on the other day."

Doris nodded. "You drove right over the spot where our house used to be. Losing that place was a terrible blow. It had been in Lee's family for generations. His great-grandfather had built it. We wanted to avoid another tragedy like that, so when we had the chance to move to Sheffield Peak, we didn't hesitate. We figured that no one would take our house from us way out here, even if we didn't own the land. But we were wrong."

She paused for a moment, her lips pressed together, then said: "A man named Somerset Fletcher owns this mountain. Lee used to work for him in Darby, maintaining his house and grounds, and sometimes he worked here, too. He sawed up fallen trees, kept the hiking trails clear, mowed fields, that sort of thing—with Clint, who was already living here. When he found out the road was taking our house, Mr. Fletcher told Lee we could live here

too if we wanted. We jumped at the offer, and haven't regretted it for a minute.

"Then a couple of weeks ago a car pulled into our dooryard. It was Mr. Fletcher's lawyer, Mr. Osterfeld. He said Mr. Fletcher had wanted to come himself but couldn't, he was too ill, then told us the land was being sold. There was going to be a ski resort built here, and we'd have to move.

"We couldn't believe it. We'd always thought Mr. Fletcher would never sell, but would pass the land onto his heirs, who'd keep it the way it had always been. But he'd learned that his heirs planned to split up the land into parcels and sell them as soon as he died. He didn't want that, and decided to sell it to someone who'd keep it whole. This way the heirs, who were strapped for cash, would get money, but not the land. He found a buyer right away who agreed not to split up the land. But now this person is building a ski resort."

She looked at the windows again, her eyes heavy and sad. "What a terrible turn of events," she said. "This land is so wild and pure, to see it commercialized…" She shook her head. "And we'll have to leave it and get an apartment, I guess, we can't afford to buy a house. Finding a good place won't be easy, the rents are so high these days. We have a little money in the bank, not much, but enough not to qualify for subsidized housing. Most of the money's from Jeff and Ellen's life insurance. We've set it aside for Ruby's college. We don't want to use it for anything else, but it looks like we're going to have to."

Her shoulders heaved as she took a breath. "Leaving this wonderful place will be terribly hard, but I guess we'll manage to cope, we've dealt with lots worse. Apartment living won't stop me from cooking and knitting and doing my crafts, and Lee will still have his carving. But we won't be able to grow our own food anymore, or cut our own wood, or keep bees, and that will hurt. Our link with the land will be broken.

"And this has me worried—for Lee. This mountain gives him

so much strength, and to move away… The Darby air, you'd think it would be quite good in a small remote country town, but sadly, that's not the case. A cement plant there fills the sky every night with dust. I saw plenty of respiratory illness at the hospital where I worked, and Lee, with his lung condition…I'm really concerned. And then, of course, there's poor old Clint—"

The door to the porch swung open, cutting her off, and Ruby and Lee appeared in the entryway, stomping their feet and shaking the snow off their clothes. Charlotte ran over to Doris and nosed her knee, did the same to Dodge, then went to the living room hearth and lay down.

"It's still snowing like crazy," Lee said as he took off his jacket. "Ruby would slide all day, but this old coot needs tea."

"And how about more of those cookies?" Doris said.

"Yes!" Ruby said. She took off her mittens and boots and snowsuit, hung up the snowsuit and washed her hands at the sink.

Doris brought cups to the table and filled them with steaming hot water while Ruby brought over the cookie tin.

Dodge asked for the tea he had drunk last night. He was getting another headache, probably caused by the absence of coffee and cigarettes.

"I went down the hill a hundred times!" Ruby said with a great big grin. Her cheeks were still red from the cold.

"Oh, not that many," Lee said. "A lot, but not that many."

"I bet it was," Ruby said. Biting into a cookie she said, "I'm going to make a Christmas card for Mr. Clint when I finish my tea. A very pretty one."

"What a nice idea," Doris said.

Lee took a swallow of tea, then, looking outside, he said with a grin, "Well, I'll be a monkey's uncle!"

They followed his gaze. A large dark shape was standing some distance away in the falling snow.

"A horse," Dodge said.

Ruby laughed. "That isn't a horse," she said. "It's a moose!"

"No kidding," Dodge said, feeling foolish. He went to the window. "I've never seen one before."

"Maybe he wants to go sliding too," Lee said.

Ruby laughed. "That's silly, Papa."

The animal lingered a minute, then walked away.

"Are there many moose here?" Dodge asked.

"Oh sure," Lee said. "We're surrounded by all kinds of wildlife: bear, coyotes, bobcats…and of course lots of deer and skunks and raccoons and groundhogs."

"I never saw a bear," Ruby said. "Or a bobcat."

"You live here long enough, you will," Lee said.

"The groundhogs eat our garden," Ruby said. "That's why Papa made the fence. I see the groundhogs sometimes. They stand right up on their two back legs. It's funny!"

Chapter 8

Gentleness will overcome
the hard and strong.
Don't show others your methods,
just show them the results.

—Tao Te Ching

They finished their snack and Dodge helped Ruby clear the table. As Doris resumed her knitting and Ruby started to make her Christmas card for Clint, Lee said, "Can you give me hand with something, Russ? No heavy lifting involved, I promise."

Dodge followed him through the kitchen and down the hall to the workshop. His head was feeling better again—thanks to the magical tea?

When they entered the workshop, Dodge was instantly confronted by his shirt and socks and underwear, which hung on the clothesline along with a lot of other stuff. He saw the potter's wheel again, a kiln, and the wall holding dozens of tools, which he looked at more closely now. There were hammers, saws, wrenches, planes, screwdrivers, chisels… He noticed no power tools at all; even the drills were the old-fashioned kind. He said, "You didn't build this cottage with *hand* tools, did you?"

"We cut the cordwood with a chainsaw. For everything else, we used hand tools. We find them more satisfying than power tools."

Dodge shook his head. "That sure was a lot of work."

"It was, but we enjoyed it."

Again, Dodge marveled at the patience these people had; they never seemed to hurry. "Great setup you got here," he said.

Lee smiled. "Sure is." With a nod at the potter's wheel he said, "This is where Doris does her ceramics. Those flower pots in the living room? The soup bowls? Soap holders? Candlesticks? Pitchers? She made them all."

"You people are just amazing."

Lee laughed. "Come here, take a look at this."

He started across the room. Dodge followed, observing how neat the workspace was; all tools were in the proper place and the floor was perfectly clean.

Lee stopped at the long workbench. "Ruby's Christmas presents," he said.

On top of the workbench, more of that wonderful dollhouse furniture: a four-poster bed, a bureau, a dresser with mirror, a bookcase and two nightstands, all of them carved from a golden wood. "Outstanding," Dodge said. "What kind of wood did you use?"

"Wild black cherry," Lee said. "I haven't walked every foot of the Peak, I guess, but I've come real close, and I've only found eight black cherries. One of the biggest blew over last spring and couldn't be saved. It was a shame to lose it, but at least I'm using it well."

"You certainly are."

"What you're looking at here," Lee said, "is the doll parents' bedroom furniture. I don't know if Doris told you, but—"

"She told me. What a tragedy."

"I'm still not sure if Ruby understands," Lee said. "Sometimes when I see her playing with her house, I think she feels that maybe they'll still come back. In her imaginary world, the parents are still alive—the parents of Amy, the girl who lives there."

"She gave me a tour of her house," Dodge said, "so I know about Amy. Her parents sleep on the floor."

Lee smiled and said, "That's right. I can't wait to see the look on her face when she opens her presents tomorrow."

"I'm sure she'll be thrilled," Dodge said—and suddenly thought of the alpine village he planned to build, its gift shop. "You ever make stuff for sale?" he asked.

"No, I'm too slow a worker to make stuff for sale. You see, no matter what I do, it has to be done *right*."

"I can relate to that."

"If I hurry," Lee said, "I'll make mistakes. As the saying goes, 'It never shows how long it took, it only shows how good you did it.'"

"Gotcha," Dodge said. But he not only wanted things done *right,* he wanted them done *fast.* "That dollhouse," he said. "I'm sure you could sell those for plenty."

Lee shrugged. "Could be, but I never do anything twice, it would ruin the fun." He opened a drawer in the workbench and said, "Take a gander at this."

Dodge saw a necklace made of round and oblong wooden beads. "What a beauty," he said.

"Pick it up."

Dodge did. "I've never seen anything like it—and it feels so smooth."

"It's made out of three kinds of birch," Lee said, "white, yellow and black. White and yellow are common, but black, that's not easy to find around here." He winked. "But I know where to find it. So this is my Christmas present for Doris."

"She'll love it," Dodge said. He was thinking that Paula would love it too—and he hadn't yet bought her a gift. Placing the necklace back in the drawer he said, "You haven't made more of these, have you?"

"Oh, sure," Lee said, "but this is a new design."

"Uh-huh. But I mean, do you have any others around? I have this friend—"

"Sorry, but no, I don't," Lee said, and he closed the drawer.

His brusque tone startled Dodge. Suggesting he wanted to buy Lee's work had offended him?

"Now here's where you'll help me save my knees," Lee said.

He went to a long tall closet across the room and opened a sliding door. "I'm going to give you some boxes," he said, unfolding a small stepladder. He started to climb.

He reached high up to the very top shelf and grabbed a box and handed it down to Dodge, who set it on the spotless floor. He handed down three more boxes, none of them heavy, and that was it. "Our Christmas ornaments," Lee said, descending the ladder.

Lee carried the largest box and Dodge carried the other three. When they entered the living room Doris was now in her chair by the fire and Ruby was on the sofa, reading. "It's time to decorate the tree!" she said. "Mommom, we have to make popcorn!"

"We certainly do," Doris said. "Go get me the corn and the popper, please."

Ruby ran to the kitchen, and soon she was back with a jar and the popper—a wire mesh basket on a rod. She opened the popper's lid and Doris poured kernels inside. "Be careful now, you don't want to burn it," she said.

"I won't," Ruby said. She slid the lid of the popper shut, pulled the fireplace screen aside, and thrust the wire basket into the flames.

Soon it was popping away and Ruby was shaking the rod and laughing. The popping slowed down and Doris said, "I think that's enough, let's see."

Ruby came over and showed it to her.

"Yes, that's fine. Set it down on the hearth and get me a bowl and my sewing basket, please."

Ruby went off again and fetched the requested items. Dumping the popcorn into the bowl, Doris asked, "Does anyone want some before I start making the strand?"

"I do," Ruby said, and dipped her hand into the bowl. Lee passed the bowl to Dodge, who wasn't hungry, but took some anyway.

He found it dry and sweet. "Sure tastes a lot better than cineplex stuff," he said.

"What does cineplex stuff taste like?" asked Ruby.

"Greasy salty paper."

"I wouldn't like that at all!" Ruby said. She put her hand into the bowl again and said, "What does 'cineplex' mean?"

"It's a place with a lot of movie theaters," Doris said.

"We bought some candy at the Grand, but not any popcorn," Ruby said.

"That's right," Doris said. "Now no more eating or I'll run short."

As she set to work with her needle and thread to make the long popcorn strand, Lee took a string of tiny lights out of one of the boxes. "Here's where we use up some of our battery power," he said. "Can you give me a hand, Russ?"

Dodge helped him place the lights on the tree, then plugged them in.

"I love the Christmas lights!" Ruby said.

"Me too," Doris said, and held up the popcorn strand.

Lee and Dodge wound it around the tree and Doris said, "That doesn't look bad at all."

"It's beautiful!" Ruby said. "Now let's do the cookies!"

She brought in the tin from the kitchen. Doris put hooks through the holes in the cookies then handed them out to the others, who hung them on the tree.

"Now the ormaments!" Ruby said.

"It's 'ornaments,' honey," Lee said.

"Okay, well where are the ones I made?"

"In the box with the blue letters on its side."

Ruby opened the box and took out some painted paper animals. "I made these last Christmas," she said. "In China, each year has an animal. This is the ox." She held it up to Dodge.

"Very nice," he said.

She carefully hung it on a branch and picked up another one. "Monkey," she said. "That's when Papa was born, in the year of the monkey, and that's why he says 'I'll be a monkey's uncle.'" She laughed.

"So that's why he says that," Dodge said.

"Yes! It's silly! Mommom was born in the year of the dog. I was born in the year of the rabbit—and I can really hop! You want to see?" She jumped, and Charlotte, standing beside her, barked.

"Very good," Dodge said.

Ruby laughed again and said, "What year was Charlotte born in, Mommom?"

"I don't know, I'd have to look it up."

"Maybe the year of the horse," Ruby said. "A dog that was born in the year of the horse, that would be *really* silly." She looked at Dodge. "What year were you born in, Mr. Russ?"

"I haven't the slightest idea," Dodge said. "You'll have to look that up too."

"Oh," Ruby said, and then, with a frown: "How come there's no year of the moose?"

"Maybe they don't have moose in China," Doris said.

"We should go there and see," Ruby said.

"Well, maybe we will someday," Lee said.

When Ruby had finished hanging up all her animals, Lee hung the ornaments he had made, with help from Dodge. Dodge hung an elf, a reindeer, a model T car, a candy cane, a tiny sled that looked like Ruby's, thinking these things would sell like hot-cakes in specialty shops in New York—or in his alpine village.

"All finished except for one thing," Lee said, "and Ruby, you know what it is."

"Yes!" Ruby said.

She went to the last unopened box and took off its lid. Gently she reached inside it and brought out a bright three dimensional star. Its many points were coated with glittering silver and gold.

"My mommy and daddy made this star," she said. "Daddy made it from real light wood called balsa wood, and Mommy painted it."

"It's the best Christmas star I've ever seen," Dodge said—and he meant it.

"They made it when I was a baby," Ruby said. "They said that *I* was their star, right, Mommom?"

"Yes," Doris said. "They did."

"I don't remember," Ruby said. "We put this star on our tree in the house where I lived with them but I don't remember that, either. I try real hard, but I can't."

"It was a long time ago," Lee said.

Ruby nodded and said, "It goes up on top, can you put it there, Mr. Russ?" She held it out.

Dodge took it—and suddenly felt a rush of emotion. *Her parents made this.* It weighed practically nothing. He placed it on top of the tree and found that his hands were quivering. "How's that look?"

"Just perfect!" Ruby said, and flashed a smile that sent a pang through his heart.

"We call it the star of peace," Lee said.

"And may we have peace throughout the coming year," Doris said.

Dodge nodded. "To peace."

Lee pulled the plug on the string of lights—"Gotta save the electric"—and took the empty boxes back to his shop.

As Doris began to make dinner, Ruby completed her work at the kitchen table. The windows were now pitch black.

"This is the card for Mr. Clint," Ruby said, and held it up.

"Well, look at Simon," Doris said. "All dressed up for Christmastime."

"Yes!" Ruby said.

Dodge had been checking Lee's model of Cordwood Cottage again; now he stood in the kitchen archway. "Who's Simon?" he asked.

Ruby showed him the card. "It's Mr. Clint's cat."

"In a Santa Claus hat?"

"It's silly," Ruby said, "but I think Mr. Clint will like it."

"I'm sure he will."

She put the card down on the table and picked up another she'd made. "This one's for you," she said.

Again Dodge felt that sweet contraction in his chest. "Why, thank you, Ruby."

"I'm the girl on the sled. If you keep this card, you'll remember me."

"Oh, I'll keep it all right," Dodge said. "And I certainly will remember you."

Ruby smiled, then started to set the table.

Lee came back and the meal was served, but what they were eating, Dodge couldn't tell. It looked like meatloaf, but wasn't.

"It's a mixture of beans and walnuts," Doris said.

Prime health nut food, Dodge thought, but it was really good. "Very tasty," he said.

This was the night that he'd planned to eat at Romulus, have one of their melt-in-your-mouth filets. The money he'd spend on a meal like that would probably feed the Hansens for over a month. In a way it seemed crazy to blow so much dough on a single dinner, but after all, he didn't run his business in order to give to charities. He ran it so he could afford to eat at five star restaurants, live in a fancy condo, own new luxury cars and buy fine clothes. Was there anything wrong with that? No way, he'd worked darn hard to get where he was. Still, when he pictured himself at Romulus, surrounded by dozens of others indulging themselves in the highest of haute cuisine, his feeling was undeniably negative. Why?

After dessert, bread pudding with wild blackberry sauce—as good as anything that Romulus would serve—Dodge helped Ruby clear the table and said he would dry the dishes.

"Of course you won't," Doris said, "you're our guest."

"But not a very helpful one, I'm afraid."

"Our guests don't have to be helpful."

"I insist."

So Doris washed, Dodge dried, and Ruby and Lee played a game called Othello at the kitchen table. Dodge didn't know the game, which seemed to be a variant of checkers, but Ruby was quite proficient at it. She beat Lee twice then said, "I want to play Mr. Russ."

Dodge hadn't played any games in years—except at Atlantic City. He played three rounds with Ruby and lost them all, and after his third defeat she said, "You're not very good."

"Hey, this is the first time I played." Dodge said. "And I'm getting better. That last game was closer, wasn't it?"

"It was. So maybe if you play a whole lot more—"

"No more tonight, Ruby Li," Doris said, "it's time for your bath."

"Already?"

"It's seven fifteen. And tomorrow is Christmas Day."

"Yes!" Ruby said. "I'll get my sleeper."

She went up the stairs, gaily humming a tune—jingle bells.

"What a kid," Dodge said.

"The best," Doris said.

In the living room, Doris and Lee took the fireplace chairs and Dodge sat on the couch. The flames bathed his body with cheerful warmth, the cat and dog were curled up near the hearth, and he felt a wonderful sense of contentment.

Ruby came down the stairs again, still humming, and holding her sleeper, a green one. Smiling, she went down the hall to the bathroom.

Doris began to knit again. Lee plugged the Christmas tree lights back in and sat there staring at the star. Charlotte decided to rouse herself and came over and stood by Dodge. He stroked her head and she closed her eyes. "You are such a good dog," Dodge said, surprised by his feelings toward her.

He thought of Paula then, far off in busy Manhattan. This wasn't the first time he'd stood her up, of course; she was probably more angry than worried. He wondered if it was snowing down in New York.

Ruby returned, her cheeks flushed from her bath, her black hair damp. When she looked at the Christmas tree, her eyes lit up. "I love the star!" she said. "I love the tree!"

Doris said, "Aren't we lucky to have it?"

"We are," Ruby said, coming over to Dodge. "I cut it with Papa out in the woods. We used a saw."

"A chainsaw?"

"No, a bow saw."

"Well, you sure picked a beauty."

"We did," Ruby said, and she looked at Doris. "Can Mr. Russ read me my story tonight?" she asked with a sunny smile.

"Sure, if he wants to," Doris said.

"Well can you, Mr. Russ?"

"I'd love to."

Ruby went to the bookcase wall. "I have so many books," she said. "*Where the Wild Things Are, Winnie the Pooh, The Little Prince…*"

"Remember what night this is," Doris said.

"Yes!" Ruby said, and searched the shelves, and came up with *The Night Before Christmas.*

She sat next to Dodge on the couch and gave him the book. When he opened it up, she snuggled close, he felt her warmth, and it gave him a sudden thrill. He smiled, then looked at the picture on the page—Santa Claus in his sleigh, laughing and waving, the reindeer pulling him through the sky. Taking a breath, he began:

"'Twas the night before Christmas—'"

"What's that mean, 'twas'," Ruby asked.

"That's an old-fashioned word for 'it was,'" Dodge said.

"Oh." Ruby snuggled in closer; again Dodge felt that thrill.

"'Twas the night before Christmas, when all through the house, not a creature was stirring, not even a mouse.'"

"We had a mouse in our kitchen once," Ruby said. "It ran across the counter, then squeezed through the tiniest hole in the floor you ever saw."

"Ruby," Doris said. "If you keep interrupting Mr. Russ, it will take him forever to read the story."

"Oh—I'm sorry."

"I really don't mind," Dodge said, and continued: "'The stockings were hung by the chimney with care—'"

"I'm going to hang my stocking later."

"Ruby," Doris said.

"Oh—I forgot."

Dodge looked at her. "Are we ready?"

"We are."

She refrained from interrupting the rest of the way. "'Happy Christmas to all, and to all a good night!'" Dodge said with a flourish.

"Yes!" Ruby said with a great big grin. "Thank you, Mr. Russ."

"You're very welcome."

Ruby slid off the couch and went to the tree. Under it lay her stocking, and she took it to the fireplace. Turning to Dodge she said, "Mr. Russ, will you lift me?"

Dodge went over and picked her up. She hung the stocking on the nail protruding from the mantelpiece and he put her down again. "Mommom made that stocking for me when I was little," she said. "She made my sleeper, too."

"I think maybe your Mommom and Papa can make anything they want," Dodge said.

"They can!" Ruby said, then abruptly she turned to the windows. "We forgot to pull the shades down," she said, "and guess what? The moon is out!"

Everyone looked, and yes, the storm had ended. "Hallelujah," Doris said.

Ruby went to the windows. "'The moon on the breast of the new-fallen snow gave the luster of midday to objects below.'"

"You remember that!" Dodge said.

"I remember the whole story," Ruby said.

"Get out."

"I do. You want to hear me say it?"

"No time for that now," Doris said. "Now it's time for bed."

"Yes! Tomorrow is Christmas!"

Ruby went over to Doris and gave her a hug, and then she hugged Lee, and then she gave Dodge a hug. She felt so soft and warm in her sleeper and gave off the sweet scent of soap. "Good night," he said.

"Good night, Mr. Russ, I'll see you in the morning. Christmas morning!"

"Sleep well," Dodge said. "Sweet dreams."

Chapter 9

These three things are treasures:
Compassion, frugality, humility.
—Tao Te Ching

Ruby went up the stairs and the house was quiet. The fire had lost its flame and was embers now. Charlotte was standing next to Dodge and he gently stroked her neck. He said, "Can she really recite that whole poem?"

"She can," Doris said. "Of course, she's probably heard it a dozen times."

"Even so, that's pretty darn good for a six year old, right?" He wasn't sure if it was or not. What did he know about six year olds?

"It sure *is* good," Lee said. He put a log on the fire and stoked the coals, then left the room. A few minutes later he reappeared with a bunch of bags and some wrapping paper.

"Well what do you know, here's Santa," Doris said.

Lee set the stuff on the kitchen table. "Better get busy, Mrs. Claus."

Doris looked over at Dodge. "Want to help us wrap?"

"I'd love to," Dodge said, "but I'm terrible at it, I always have the store do it. I'll watch you, though, and maybe I'll learn a few tricks."

All of them sat at the table. Doris and Lee took things out of the bags and put them in boxes and wrapped with calm efficiency: the dollhouse furniture Dodge had seen in the workshop, books, clothes, crayons, drawing paper... They took it all into the living room and placed it under the tree.

Dodge went back to the couch as Doris filled Ruby's stocking with little gifts: a bag of marbles, a dog and cat made from cloth, some card games, a packet of almond paste cookies, a word find magazine.

"She loves finding words," Doris said. "She loves to read."

"And already wants to be a doctor," Dodge said.

"She's wanted to be a doctor ever since she came to live with us," Lee said. "She'd make a good one, too, I bet, but medical school...no way we could ever pay for that."

"If she really wants to go, she will," Doris said. "She'll work her way through, she's a very determined child."

"She's something, all right," Dodge said.

"She's our star."

"That's plain to see."

"She saved us," Lee said.

Dodge frowned at him. "What do you mean?"

"She pulled us out of our grief. We had no time to wallow in our despair—because of her."

Doris said, "As I told you before, we were babysitting Ruby that tragic night. I was reading her a bedtime story when the telephone rang. Lee answered it. All he kept saying was 'yes,' but I instantly knew there was something terribly wrong. He hung up the phone and said, 'That was the state police. There's been an

accident'—and I knew what had happened. I said to Ruby, 'We'll finish this story tomorrow.' She looked confused and asked me why. 'Because Mommom is tired now,' I said, and Ruby, bless her heart, just said okay, and I took her upstairs and tucked her in bed and hugged her with tears in my eyes. And then I went down, and Lee confirmed what I already knew, and we held each other and wept. And just kept weeping, for Jeff and Ellen, and for ourselves, and most of all for poor little Ruby.

"We lay awake all night. In the morning I heard Ruby stir and I went to her room. "Where's Mommy and Daddy?" she asked, and what could I do, I had to tell her, and so I did, holding her in my arms. At first she looked puzzled, and then she wept. 'I want my mommy," she kept on saying, over and over again. 'I want my daddy.'

"Finally she stopped, and I gave her some cereal. I couldn't eat. She said, 'Will Mommy and Daddy come back soon?' As gently as I could, I told her no, and it broke my heart to say it. 'Will they come home tomorrow?' she'd ask, and we'd tell her again. Again and again and again—they would never come back."

Doris looked at the fire; her eyes were moist. She turned to Dodge again. "There are books," she said, "for us and for children as well, and we spoke to some people who deal with these situations—therapists and hospice workers. All of it helped a little, I guess, but what can you really say to a three year old about death?" She shook her head. "If Lee had still been a paramedic, he might have responded to the call. We were spared that, at least."

Lee looked down at the floor, at the braided rug. "We wanted Jeff back so much," he said. "Our only child, gone forever, and Ellen... Three years ago, and the hurt hasn't stopped, and I guess it never will. But we've kept on going, and *will* keep going. We have to, for Ruby's sake."

Doris nodded. "For months she would wake in the night crying, 'Want my mommy. Want my daddy,' echoing what was in our hearts, and I would go in and hold her. Now she almost never asks about them anymore. It's almost like they were characters in a story. She looks at that picture of them there on the table, sometimes she looks at the albums we have, but what does she really remember? She came to them at the age of fourteen months and lived with them only two years."

"She's so sensitive though," Lee said. "So perceptive. One time I was in this room alone, just staring at Jeff and Ellen's wedding picture, and Ruby came in. I was lost in thought and didn't hear her. Suddenly she said to me, 'Oh, Papa, don't be sad.' It tore me up."

"The hurt is still there inside her," Doris said. "Back in the spring I had to go spend the night at the home of a friend who was sick. As I walked out the door Ruby asked, "Will I ever see you again?"

Dodge said nothing, just shook his head.

Doris looked at the fire again and said, "We're not the kind of people who worry a lot about things that will probably never happen. It's a fine way to ruin your life. And despite all the terrible things we'd seen in the course of our jobs, we never imagined a blow like this would strike us. We never imagined we'd be where we are today, but…here we are. Somewhere along the line we all learn life is harder than we ever dreamed—and we're stronger than we ever dreamed."

She sighed. "Well, enough of the past, it's Christmas Eve, a time of hope, a time to think of the future." She looked at the tree and the presents beneath it. "I'd say the Clauses did a real fine job. All three of them."

Lee stood up and went to her and kissed her on the cheek. "I'm going out to look at that gorgeous moon before I turn in," he said. "Does anyone care to join me?"

"I'll join you," Dodge said.

The air was piercingly cold and perfectly clear, and the sky was filled with thousands of shimmering stars.

"What a sight," Dodge said.

"Once you're away from the city lights," Lee said, "you can really see what's going on up there. And on nights when there isn't any moon, well, you should see it *then*. You know, it's just as magical to me today as it was when I was a kid."

Dodge tried to think of when he had last taken time to look at the stars—to *really* look. He couldn't remember them ever as sharp and numerous as this. One of them in particular caught his eye and he said, "That star near the moon, it's so *bright*."

"Actually," Lee said, "that's Venus."

"Oh, of course," Dodge said, trying to mask his embarrassment.

"On a night like this," Lee said, "you really know where you stand in the scheme of creation. We're here on this little planet for such a short time, even those of us lucky enough to live to old age. May we earn the wisdom to use our allotment well." He looked at the valley, the conifers covered with snow and silvered with moonlight. "Well, now that the storm is over," he said, "they'll plow the roads, and tomorrow we'll get you out of here."

"That's great," Dodge said. Then he quickly added, "I've really enjoyed my stay."

"Well, you'll come back and visit us one of these days I hope," Lee said, "but don't wait too long. Once they develop this mountain, we're gone—and this beautiful land is gone." He let out a deep breath, white in the frosty air. "Well, there's nothing that Doris and I can do about that," he said.

Dodge stared at the valley, the crisp cold light on the trees. "But maybe you won't have to move," he said. "Maybe the people who buy the mountain will let you stay here."

Lee shook his head. "Yes, maybe," he said. "But the problem is, it won't be 'here' anymore. The Peak as we've always known it will vanish." He looked at the valley and said, "I owe my life to this place, it restored my health."

Dodge could believe it. His breathing was just so *easy* here.

Lee looked at the stars again and said, "I'm glad that Ruby has had the chance to see the Peak as it is today, but she probably won't remember much, she's so young." He shrugged. "Well, that's how it goes."

As they started back to the porch, Lee said, "We get our water from a stream. Can you imagine what the golf course runoff will do to that?"

They went inside, and Doris asked, "You boys want anything to eat before I go to bed? Some cookies?"

They both said no, and Lee said, "Doris, I have a job to do in my shop, but I'll join you soon."

"A job at this hour? On Christmas Eve?"

"Just something small that I want to take care of," Lee said, and he gave her a little kiss."

"Well don't stay up real late."

"I won't."

The two of them looked at the tree for a minute. "Can't wait till tomorrow," Lee said. "Me neither," said Doris, then said goodnight and went up the stairs.

Lee turned to Dodge and whispered, "I need to go wrap her present."

Dodge nodded, smiling, and Lee went down the hallway to his shop.

Dodge sat on the couch and looked at the fireplace, feeling its radiant warmth. He looked at the stocking hanging there, bulging with tiny presents. He looked at the Christmas tree and thought of the necklace that Lee had made. Three different kinds of birch. Dodge didn't know a spruce from a pine; to him they were all just Christmas trees. And what kind of tree was this one here, this beautiful tree with the star on top? He didn't have any idea, and thought: That's kind of pathetic.

The star was now shining with light from the tiny bulbs, making him think of the stars outside, and it seemed to hold some of their magic.

He looked at the table beside him, the photograph there: the smiling young couple, the people who'd made that star.

He looked at the other photo, of three year old Ruby—their star. He sighed, then, followed by Charlotte, his good friend now, he went to his room.

Chapter 10

If you honor the world as you
honor yourself
you can nurture the world.

—Tao Te Ching

Dodge awoke to the sound of voices. The windows in his room were still pitch black.

He couldn't make out what Ruby was saying, but she was clearly excited. He hurriedly put on his robe and went to the living room.

The fire was blazing, Doris and Lee were in their chairs, and Ruby, still in her bright green sleeper, was opening presents. She'd already dumped her stocking's contents onto the floor's rag rug.

"Mr. Russ!" she said. "I got a bed for the Mommy and Daddy's room!" and she held it up. "They don't have to sleep on the floor anymore!"

"I'm sure they'll appreciate that," Dodge said with a smile.

"And look, a dresser, too—with a mirror! And a bureau!" She opened one of the little drawers, her face delighted.

"Isn't that super."

"Yes!"

She opened another package. "A sweater!" she said. It was made out of wool: red, yellow and blue. "Thank you, Mommom. Thank you for making it for me."

"How did you know I made it?" Doris said.

Ruby just laughed.

Dodge thought of his childhood Christmases. He'd gotten a lot more presents than Ruby, but hadn't been nearly as happy with them.

Ruby had made some presents too: a drawing of Charlotte for Lee and a small box covered with colorful stones for Doris.

"I think I know what would fit in that box just right," Lee said, giving Doris her gift.

Doris opened the little package. "Oh Lee, how lovely," she said, holding the necklace up. "Three kinds of birch, am I right?"

Lee laughed. "Are you ever wrong?"

She put it on and Ruby said, "It's beautiful!"

"It couldn't be more beautiful," Doris said. "Well, Lee, we'll have to do some stepping out and show it off."

"We'll hit all the night spots," Lee said with another laugh.

Doris said, "Ruby, give Papa that box with the silver ribbon. The red one."

"This?" Ruby said as she held it up.

"That's it."

The box contained three pairs of heavy wool socks—gray, purple and red—that Doris had knitted. "If these don't keep the ice away from my toes then nothing will," Lee said.

Doris asked Ruby to give Mr. Russ a box that sat on the hearth. Taken aback, Dodge said. "What's this?"

"Well, open it up and find out," Doris said.

Dodge unwrapped the package—and there was the purple scarf he'd seen Doris knitting the day before—and a black wool cap. "Well…thank you very much," he said.

As soon as he wrapped the scarf around his neck he heard a rumbling, grinding noise outside. "It's Jerry!" Ruby said.

"Yep, we're getting plowed out," Lee said. He pulled up the quilted shades at the windows then went to the door and put on his jacket. "Gotta wish him a Merry Christmas."

Dodge watched the plow bite into the deep soft snow, again and again, pushing it into high hills. It turned around, its lights flashing into the living room briefly, then stopped. Lee spoke to the driver, who nodded and then took off.

Lee came inside again. As he hung up his jacket he said, "I told Jerry your situation, Russ. He'll come back later to take you to Darby, after his plowing's done—sometime this afternoon. Everything's closed today but you can hang out at the inn and make your calls, and tomorrow you'll rent a car at the Chevy place. Jerry will have your wreck towed out when he has the time."

"Lee, that's great news," Dodge said.

As dawn lit the hills to the east, they all had a breakfast of pancakes with blueberry syrup. By the time they finished, the sun was diamond-sharp on the snow and the cottage was flooded with light.

Dodge took another bath and shaved, then put on his nice clean underwear and his slacks and shirt. When he came back into the kitchen, Doris was busily cooking, but Ruby and Lee were gone.

"They went to see Clint," Doris said. "We hope he can join us for dinner, we're eating at one. Jerry won't come for you until we're done, I'm sure, he's got a zillion customers."

As Doris worked, Dodge took another look at the paintings beside the door. The light reflecting off the snow made them seem more alive than ever. He went to the living room and looked at those paintings too, at Lee's carvings, the afghans and pillows that Doris had made. He looked at the cordwood walls, the fireplace, the pots on the window shelf, the rug on the floor. What skills these people had! He himself was a guy who needed to call a plumber to fix a dripping faucet, a guy with only one special skill—a knack for buying and selling. And really, he thought, what kind of a skill is that?

Ruby came bursting through the door with the happy news that birds were at the feeder. "Two juncos and a chickadee!" she said.

"And tell Mr. Russ what they're eating," Lee said.

"They're eating the sunflower seeds I grew."

"So you're a farmer too," Dodge said.

"A little bit. I grow flowers and lettuce and radishes. *White* radishes."

"White radishes. Are they Chinese?"

"They are. And they're big!" She spread her hands apart.

"I'll have to come back in the summer and eat one."

"Yes, you will!"

Doris checked one of the pots on the stove and said to Lee, "I assume Clint will join us today."

Lee laughed. "He says he will—if he can manage to clear a good path to our house. He'll try it, too, if I don't hurry—see you in a bit." He turned and went outside again.

"The snow is this deep!" Ruby said, putting her hands on her hips.

"I can't be *that* deep," Doris said. "You wouldn't be able to walk."

"But I did! I'm strong."

Doris laughed, and Ruby went outside again with Charlotte.

Dodge dressed in his brand new scarf and hat, the jacket and boots and mittens, then went to the porch. The three little black and white birds on the feeder—they all looked the same to Dodge—departed at his approach. Grabbing the extra shovel, he caught up to Lee and worked beside him while Ruby and Char-

lotte went sliding again. As old as Lee was and with only one lung, he moved more snow than Dodge. It was humiliating, but Dodge felt good. Unlike his health club workouts, this exercise was purposeful, satisfying. And his leg hardly hurt at all.

Sun dazzled the snow on the trees in the valley as far as the eye could see and the sky was pure endless blue. Amazed by Lee's stamina, Dodge worked hard. He was filled with a sense of freedom, and thought he knew why. He was someone who never really took time off; on "vacation" he was always tied to the cellphone and e-mail, constantly doing business. Here, for the first time in years, he was disconnected.

He couldn't see Sheffield Road in the sparkling valley, but now up ahead he could see Clint's cabin. Warm in his Christmas scarf and hat, he shoveled alongside Lee without saying a word, and soon they were at the door.

Lee knocked. After a minute the door came open, revealing a short wiry man with a thick gray beard. He was wearing a faded and frayed gray sweatshirt with large blue letters—"UMA"—a college? on its front. Lee introduced Dodge as they stepped inside. Clint had them sit at his table and offered them coffee, which they declined.

Dodge looked around. As far as he could tell, the place consisted of only one room, with a cot below one of the windows, a table, four chairs, a sink, a small woodstove, and a tiny fridge. Now *this* is a camp, he thought. But everything was perfectly clean and tidy: no dishes in the sink, no dirt on the floor, no clothes on the backs of the chairs. A yellow cat on the windowsill—the famous Simon, certainly—but no cat smell.

Clint said to Dodge, "They pull your car out yet?" His voice was strong, not an old man's voice.

"Not yet," Dodge said. "But I guess it's too wrecked to drive anyway."

Clint nodded. "Remember that woman went off last year?" he said as he looked at Lee. "You ever hear from her again?"

107

"Sure did, she sent us a Christmas card."

"From Ohio, right?"

"That's right."

They talked for a bit about local affairs, then Clint said, "You shoveled the path out good, I'll be able to walk to your place real easy."

"We'll see you at one then," Lee said, and he and Dodge left.

Ruby and Charlotte were still having fun on the hill. "What energy," Dodge said.

"She can go all day," Lee said.

When Dodge got back to the cottage he went to his room and lay down. He'd ache all over tomorrow from all that work, but he had enjoyed it—and needed it. He felt terrific, better than he had in years.

A knock on the door woke him up and then he heard Ruby's voice. "Mr. Russ, it's time to eat."

"Coming," he said.

He used the bathroom, splashed cold water on his face, then went to the kitchen. Clint had arrived, and he and Lee and Ruby were already there at the table. The turkey sat on a platter, surrounded by bowls of mashed potatoes, carrots, winter squash and roasted onions. Dodge took a seat and Doris did too, and Lee raised his glass of grape juice high and said, "To Christmas!"

"To Christmas!" everyone said, and clinked their glasses together and Doris said, "To our guests, Clint and Russ," and they drank.

Doris was wearing a cream-colored sweater now, and the brand new necklace—gorgeous—hung around her neck. She said, "It must be very hard for you, Russ, to be apart from your loved ones at Christmastime, but soon you'll be reunited."

"I'm enjoying my stay here very much," Dodge said, thinking: *loved ones*. Paula was the only person who fit into that category. The *only* one.

The feast began, and Clint told stories about his encounters with various wild creatures including—he swore—a cougar. He spoke of his hopes for a better crop of grapes in the coming year, then voiced his concerns about what would happen when the Peak changed hands. "Will somebody make us leave our house?" Ruby asked with a worried expression. "We hope not, but we'll have to wait and see," Lee said.

They all had herbal tea and pumpkin and apple pie. Clint had grown the pumpkins and raised the turkey. "Without you, we wouldn't have much of a dinner," Doris said.

Clint laughed. "Without you, I wouldn't have much of one either."

Suddenly Jerry's truck appeared in the dooryard. "Looks like your ride is early, Russ," Lee said.

Dodge got up from the table as Jerry came through the door. He was a burly man with a thick black beard and a ready smile. Doris invited him for dessert but he said he had too much work to do to sit right now. "But save me a piece of that punkin," he said, "and I'll stop back tomorrow."

"I'll save you a whole pie," Doris said. "You'll need it after today."

Dodge took the scarf that Doris had made and wrapped it around his neck, then put on the black wool cap.

"You're gonna want more than that," Lee said, and went to the coat rack. "Take this shirt." It was heavy and green.

"I just have to walk from the house to the truck," Dodge said.

"I want you to take it," Lee said. "You never know what might happen."

You got that right, Dodge thought. He thanked Lee, put the green shirt on, adjusted his purple scarf, and then it was time to go. Lee shook his hand and Clint did too, and Doris gave him a hug. Then he knelt to hug Ruby, and after she hugged him she said with a smile, "I want to give you a kiss."

She did, on his cheek, and a tingle went through him. "What a wonderful kiss," he said.

As he went to the door she said, "Come back for Chinese New Year's, Mommom makes her special dumplings then."

"I bet they're super."

"They are!"

"Well when is Chinese New Year's?"

Ruby turned to Doris. "When is it, Mommom?"

"Not until February."

"I'll probably be back before then," Dodge said. "If it's okay with you."

"You're welcome anytime," Lee said.

Smiling, Dodge said, "Thanks, Lee." Then Ruby said, "Mommom, the bag!"

"Good heavens, yes," said Doris. "Thank you for reminding me. Tell Mr. Russ what we call you, Ruby."

"Your memory," Ruby said.

"Without you, we'd forget to put on our pants in the morning."

"You wouldn't!" Ruby said. She laughed, then went to the counter and picked up a paper bag, which she gave to Dodge.

"What's this?" he said.

"It's cake!"

"My special Christmas cake," said Doris.

"But Doris, I can't take that."

"I made a bunch of them," Doris said. "And this one's for you."

"Well, thank you very much."

"Look in the bag," Lee said, breaking into a grin.

There was something there on top of the foil-wrapped cake, and Dodge took it out: a wooden pin in the shape of a star.

"For your lady friend," Lee said. "I didn't have time to make a necklace last night, so I hope this will do."

Dodge was astonished. "Lee, what can I say, it's beautiful. Black cherry, right?"

"Correct," Lee said.

Proud of himself, Dodge smiled. "Paula will love it."

"She will!" Ruby said. "*I* love it!" She suddenly frowned. "Do you have my card?"

"Your card! I left it in the bedroom."

"I'll get it!" Ruby said.

She was back in a flash and handed it to him.

"I'm very glad you remembered it, Ruby. Thank you very much."

"You're welcome. You'll come back soon?"

"I certainly will."

"Well, it better be soon," Lee said, "or we might not be here anymore."

Dodge shook his head. "You said you don't worry about things that might never happen, right? Big projects take years to get underway sometimes."

"I sure hope this one does," Lee said. "But from what I hear, the guy who's buying the Peak is a hotshot hustler who acts real fast."

"Oh, really," Dodge said. "Well, still, just try not to worry."

Everyone went outside to the porch except for Autumn, the cat, who stayed on the sofa. Holding the card and the paper bag, Dodge went to the truck with Jerry. He sat in the passenger seat and rolled down the window and said, "I owe you people some really big Christmas presents."

"No you don't," Doris said.

"Oh yes, I owe you plenty, and I'll be back."

"Good!" Ruby said, and Jerry started the engine. He turned the pickup truck around and started down the lane. When Dodge looked over his shoulder he saw Charlotte jumping, and Ruby, small on the porch, in sunlight, waving goodbye.

Chapter 11

Those who are content with what they have possess true wealth.

—Tao Te Ching

"They're wonderful people," Jerry said as he drove along Sheffield Road. "I don't know how many lives Lee saved when he was a paramedic, he was the best. And Doris, she was a nurse for years at Darby Regional, so she saved plenty too. And she served on the school board, the library board, she started the food bank… Every time you turned around, she was there to help. Nobody ever had anything bad to say about Doris and Lee. He was a city councilor, a volunteer fireman…

"So here you have people who grow stuff for folks who don't have enough to eat, make toys and clothing for kids at Christmastime, and what happens to them? The worst. It just ain't right, you know? I mean why did *they* have to get hit like that? Why good people like *them*? All those lives they saved, and there was nothing they could do to save their son and daughter-in-law. It's sad. They're doing a wonderful job with the little girl, but it's gotta be hard at their age. Still, they never complain—about anything. At least I've never known them to, and I've known them all my life. And now the Peak's being sold, the place that keeps them going, and they'll have to move back to town, I guess. It's gonna hit them hard—*real* hard. And Old Clint, what will happen to *him?*"

They drove by trees and fields and rooftops bright with snow, and Dodge thought Ruby was probably out on her sled again, speeding down the hill near the cottage with Charlotte in close pursuit.

They passed a Chevy place on the edge of town and Jerry said, "I'll have the car you wrecked towed here and they'll rent you another one. They ain't open today, of course, but tomorrow they open at seven. The inn can give you a lift and you'll be all set."

When they pulled up in front of the Fireside Inn, Dodge reached for his wallet, but Jerry said quickly, "No charge. Not for friends of the Hansens, no way."

"But you're going to arrange for the towing…"

"Forget it."

Dodge checked in, then went to the cigarette machine and bought a pack. In his room he put Ruby's card and the bag containing the cake and wooden pin on the desk, then sat in the chair. With eager anticipation, almost a sense of relief, he lit up.

 The cigarette tasted terrible, bitter. The pack was stale? Or did being away from smoking a couple of days make it taste that bad. Could that be possible? He crushed it out.

He had stayed at this inn—when was it, three days ago? It seemed as if a month had passed since then.

He stared out the window, remembering back to that time he had bought the Jersey condos. He'd been thrilled, but the feeling had quickly worn off, so he'd bought the mall. Same thing: way up, way down. Then Tamarack, on beautiful Willow Lake, with a fabulous owner's suite—which he practically never used, he was always so busy. And now he'd bought Sheffield Peak and would build a ski resort. Would that do it, would that be enough? Would *anything* be enough?

Aside from his major projects he had a number of smaller ones: a row of shops in Woodstock, New York; an apartment building in Philadelphia; another in Boca Raton, and there was always something going on that had to be attended to. One of his favorite sayings was "It never stops." It was a joke; he didn't really *want* it to stop. But up on the Peak, with the Hansens, it *had* stopped. And it had felt good. Now it was starting up again, and he asked himself, Isn't your plate already full enough? Maybe a bit *too* full?

He stared at the snow-covered hills in the distance, the crystalline sky, which, according to Doris, was nowhere as clean as it looked. Then, turning away from the window, he picked up the phone and called about flights to New York.

The first available plane was at ten forty-five tomorrow. He reserved a seat, then called the car rental agency.

"The accident was two days ago?" the female voice on the line said testily. "Why didn't you call before this?" He explained in detail, but when he hung up, the woman still sounded ticked off.

He called Paula, and this time she answered. Her tone was close to frantic. Where had he been? Why hadn't he called before? If she hadn't heard from him by tonight, she'd have notified the police.

He explained.

"An accident," she said. "I knew it, I just *knew* it. Thank heavens you weren't badly hurt. And you're getting the land."

"Well, no, I'm not getting the land."

"But the message you left on my phone…"

"I was wrong, I jumped the gun."

"Oh Russ, that's awful, you must be *tremendously* disappointed."

Dodge looked at Ruby's card on the desktop, the girl on the sled. "Actually," he said, "I think it's all for the best."

"But you said your heart was set on it."

"It was, but it's not anymore."

Paula was silent and Dodge said, "Instead of a mountain, I'm getting a dog."

"You're what?" Paula said. "But I thought you didn't *like* dogs."

"I didn't, but I like them now."

"What's *happened* to you?"

"I'll tell you all about it when I get back."

After he hung up the phone he went downstairs to the bar and ordered a dry martini. It tasted good, but burned when he swallowed. For the first time in days, he wanted a stomach pill, but of course they were in the wrecked car.

He looked at the Christmas tree that only a couple of days before had made him feel melancholy. This time the sight of it gladdened his heart. He thought of Ruby opening presents, the joy on her face.

He went back to his room. The desk held a folder with stationery, paper and envelopes. He took up the pen that sat beside them and started to write. When he finished he went downstairs again and had a light supper, a beer and a sandwich. He didn't feel like smoking afterward.

Back in his room he sat in the chair and turned on the news. The TV seemed terribly strident and harsh, flashing with blaring color, exhorting him to buy, buy, buy. He watched for fifteen minutes—the weather report said tomorrow would be a fine day—then turned it off. He thought of the peace at Cordwood Cottage: Ruby playing and drawing, Doris and Lee talking quietly next to the fireplace, Autumn and Charlotte warming themselves on the hearth. *Hotshot hustler*, he said to himself, and laughed.

He read the magazine that came with the room, about travel in Maine, and soon he was very sleepy and went to bed.

《《←—→》》

He was up very early; the windows were dark. As he waited for the hotel van outside the entryway, his shoulders ached from all the shoveling he'd done. But that was okay; as a matter of fact, it was fine. The moon was down, the last of the stars were fading away, and he thought of standing with Lee looking up at the sky.

By the time the van let him off at the Chevy dealer, the sky was a pale grayblue, presaging a beautiful day. He rented a car and started off, not toward Route 48 but toward Sheffield Road. When he reached the lane that led to the Hansens' place, the sun was casting a rose-colored glow on the banks of plowed snow on the road's narrow shoulder.

Dodge pulled over and looked at the little lane. An alpine village, he said to himself. What in the world was I thinking? What's going in here is a *guardrail*.

He pictured the cozy cottage, invisible from here, and the people who gave it life. They had all finished breakfast now, no doubt, and Ruby was doing her schoolwork. And when she had finished, she'd bring in the wood, and play with her dollhouse, and dream of the day when she would become a doctor and help people stay alive.

Dodge left the car and walked to the lane. He couldn't see any signs of the car he had wrecked; it was totally buried in snow. Well Jerry, bless his heart, would take care of that.

He was wearing Lee's heavy green shirt on top of his thin dress shirt, and took it off. He spread it across the mailbox, then opened the mailbox door and put an envelope inside, the envelope holding the papers he'd written the night before.

He got back in the car. The Christmas cake that Doris had made, the pin that Lee had made and the card that Ruby had made all sat on the seat beside him. He looked at them, smiling, looked back at the mailbox, and then he went on his way.

Chapter 12

The more the wise man gives to others
the more he has.

—Tao Te Ching

J ust before noon, as glorious sunlight spangled the snow-bent trees, Lee walked down the lane to get the mail with Charlotte trailing behind.

He was startled to see his old green shirt draped over the mailbox. He flung it across his arm, then opened the door of the box.

He found two solicitations for credit cards, a bill from the gas company, and an envelope from the Fireside Inn, bearing no postage stamp. It said, "FOR LEE AND DORIS AND RUBY. IMPORTANT."

"Now what in the world do you think this can be, Charlotte?" Lee said aloud. He was eager to see what the envelope held, but refrained from looking inside; after all, it was not addressed solely to him. Holding it tightly, he walked back up to the cottage.

Doris was at the table knitting and Ruby was drawing a picture. Charlotte went over to Ruby, who stroked her neck.

Lee put the mail on the table, then hung up his heavy green shirt. With a frown Doris said, "Lee, how did you get that back?"

"Russ left it on top of the mailbox."

Lee hung up his jacket and cap and took off his boots and sat down. "He left that on top of the mailbox and left this inside." He put on his dime-store reading glasses and picked up the envelope from the inn. "It's a message for all three of us."

Ruby ran over and stood beside him. "Let's see!" she said.

Withdrawing the envelope's contents, Lee said, "Well, looks like it's more than one message. This one says, 'Read this page first.' Okay, I will."

"'I just want to thank you again for all you did for me, which is more than you can possibly imagine. I will never forget your kindness. Enclosed are some belated Christmas presents. I will be back to see you soon. I owe you a toothbrush, and want to taste some of those special dumplings! Until we meet again, be well. Sincerely, Russ Dodge.'"

Ruby's face lit up. "Mr. Russ will come back soon?"

"That's what he says."

"Good! I want him to! But where are the Christmas presents?"

"I guess they're paper presents," Lee said. "Let's see. 'Read this page second.' Ruby peered over his shoulder as he said:

"'This document entitles Lee and Doris Hansen and Ruby Li Han-sen to reside in their beautiful home on Sheffield Peak, which will soon become part of the Northern Mountains Land Trust, for as long as they wish. It would be great if they would continue to care for the land as they always have, but they are under no obligation to do so. This entitlement also applies to Clint Ferguson.'"

Lee looked at Doris, frowning, shaking his head, and then he continued reading. "'You see, I'm the hotshot hustler you've heard about, the guy who bought the Peak.'"

Lee suddenly burst out laughing. "Well I'll be a monkey's uncle," he said, "isn't this something!"

"Oh, Lee," Doris said, and her eyes turned bright with tears.

"There are two more pages," Lee said, and he started to read again.

"'This document entitles Lee and Doris Hansen and Ruby Li Han-sen to one round trip to China, all expenses paid, whenever they want to go and for however long they want to stay. This voucher is renewable upon request.'"

"We can go to *China?*" Ruby said, her dark eyes wide.

"We can," Doris said, wiping away her tears with her fingers, "and we will."

"Prime!" Ruby said.

Lee and Doris laughed. And then Lee said, "This last page is just for you, Ruby."

"Just for *me?*"

"That's what it says, so listen carefully."

"'This document entitles Ruby Li Han-Sen to attend the college and medical school of her choice, all expenses paid. But in order to make good this contract, she must agree to the following condition: The next time she sees Mr. Russ, which will be real soon, she must give him another big hug and kiss.'"

Lee looked at Ruby. "Well," he said, "will you do that? Give Mr. Russ a hug and a kiss?"

"Yes!" Ruby said with a happy grin. "I will!"

She jumped, and Charlotte barked.

The End

Author

CHRISTOPHER FAHY is the author of fifteen books, among them *Limerock: Maine Stories* and the novels *Breaking Point*, *Chasing the Sun* and *Red Tape*. His stories, poems, articles and reviews have appeared in *Down East, Transatlantic Review, Puckerbrush Review, The Beloit Poetry Journal, The Twilight Zone Magazine* and many other publications. He has won the Maine Arts Commission Chapbook Award in Fiction, a grand prize in *Atlanta Review's* International Poetry Competition, and has received the Distinguished Achievement Award from the University of Maine at Augusta. Overlook Connection Press has previously published Fahy's novel *Fever 42* and a collection of his fantasy stories, *Matinee at the Flame.*

Illustrator

CORTNEY SKINNER's illustrations and paintings appear in books, magazines, films, and private collections. His work covers an extensive range of subjects including science fiction, fantasy, history, children's books, landscapes, and still lifes. He has created artworks in a variety of mediums and styles encompassing formal portraiture, representational illustration, cartoons, and sculptural work. Cortney shares life and abode in the Virginia's Shenandoah Valley with writer Elizabeth Massie.

Chinese Character Interpreter

WENJING WANG was born in Beijing, China and earned her degree in Journalism from Renmin University of China and an MFA from the Ecole Nationale Supérieure d'Art de Bourges in France. She worked several years as a photographer, editor, and translator for the international press in China. Her award-winning photography, installations, and sculptures have been exhibited in Europe and Asia as well as in many international publications. She currently lives and studies in Paris, Bourges and Beijing.

A note from the illustrator:

Each illustration in *The Christmas Star* contains a single character from the Chinese language integrated within the artwork.

The meaning of each character is pertinent to the quote from the Tao Te Ching at the beginning of each chapter.

To choose the characters, I worked with Wenjing Wang, a Beijing-born, professional translator, artist, and journalist. She examined Chinese language versions of the Tao Te Ching to find various characters and meanings that harmonized with the themes in each chapter quote as well as the text within the story. I then merged each Chinese character that we selected into the appropriate illustration. I hope you have fun finding the characters!

The Chinese characters, the chapters in which they are found, and their meanings are listed below.

Chapter 1 - greed 贪

Chapter 2 - mindfulness 善

Chapter 3 - do nothing 无

Chapter 4 - to do with patience 徐

Chapter 5 - unmoving, calm, peace 安

Chapter 6 - right, true 大

Chapter 7 - hard, difficult 难

Chapter 8 - reveal, show the result 示

Chapter 9 - treasure 宝

Chapter 10 - nature 然

Chapter 11 - enough, plenty 足

Chapter 12 - love 爱

CPSIA information can be obtained at www.ICGtesting.com
Printed in the USA
LVOW011500131212

311411LV00002BA/5/P